Rabbit Island
Nurse Practitioner:
The Thumb Drive

Linda Q. Thede

Linda Q. Thede

ISBN: 979-8-9908116-6-9

Linda Q. Thede

Map of Rabbit Island

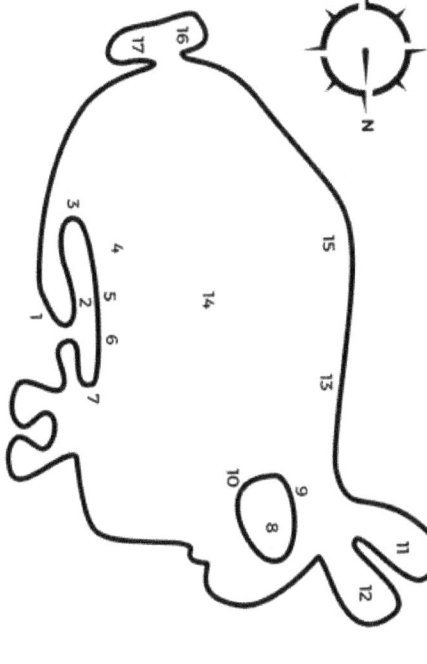

N

1. Lighthouse
2. Harbor
3. Ferry Dock
4. Rabbit Island Health Clinic
5. Fisherman's Hole
6. Busted Jip
7. Nelson's Marina
8. Lake Nanabush
9. Outlook

10. Amphitheater seen from Outlook
11. Rabbit Island Resort
12. Rabbit Island Resort Golf Course
13. Cliff House
14. Reverie in the Woods
15. Airport
16. Miss Maggie's House
17. Alex's House

CONTENTS

ACKNOWLEDGMENTS

A book is never the product of one person but of friends and relatives who give of their time. Cathy Bass's and Jane McBride's sharp eyes found many errors critical to the book. My thanks to AnnaLouise Scandiffio, who identified a missing piece of the plot. My son, Douglas, did a final edit of the book, offering many helpful suggestions. Any errors, now, are the fault of the author.

1 A BUSINESS CARD

"Javier has given us an ultimatum. Find that thumb drive or else," one of Javier's cartel enforcers told Eduardo as the two were slowly drinking their beers. "He's still upset that instead of bringing Marco to him for interrogation, we killed him. Unfortunately, Lorenzo, one of his favorites, was also killed during that battle."

"We didn't do that," Eduardo interrupted loudly." "It was that rat Marco running away from us."

"Whatever," Federico replied, "Marco had that thumb drive, which he copied from the cartel's computer. If that information got into the hands of either the feds or one of our rivals, it would be bad news. I'd love to know how he could copy that information to his thumb drive. Javier only found out because the copying left a trail. Marco must have known that and disappeared as soon as he had the information.

"That is not our concern. Our problem is finding that thumb drive or disappearing permanently, hopefully not as corpses.

Federico's brow furled as he wrestled with the problem. Suddenly, he said, "After I cut Marco's GI tract open to try and find the drive, I remember seeing a business card from some nurse near his body. I have no idea how or why it was there, but I memorized it to take my mind off what I was doing. I think I remember. It read, 'Alexandra M. Lawson, DNP, RN,

CNP, Cobury Health Clinic, Cobury, Maryland, affiliated with Eastern Maryland Medical Center.'"

"Why is this important?" Eduardo asked. "You can't think she has it or knows where it is. We don't even know how or why he had the card."

"Agreed, but what else do we have? Why don't we tell Javier we just remembered the card and we believe the woman named on it has the drive. He will tell us to find her, get that drive, and not care how we do it."

"We're still grasping at straws."

"Yes," Federico replied, "But it's all we have. As you recall, we had located Marco and had someone in Honolulu following him. We wanted to have him picked up there, but our man only found him when he was at the gate and walking aboard. The place was loaded with cops, and it would have created a scene. Then we would not only have lost him, but the drive would have gone to the FBI. Our man saw him board that flight, but was not on it when it reached Chicago. We heard the other passengers saying the flight had diverted to San Francisco for an emergency. Marco must have left it then. Otherwise, we would have captured him in Chicago."

"But that does not explain how he had her business card?"

"Let's assume she was on that flight, and he gave her the thumb drive for temporary safekeeping. Then she gave him her business card so he could get it back. And remember, we had that battle with Marco in Maryland. Why else would he be there except to retrieve the drive?"

"Assuming this is so, how do we find her?"

"I will call the Cobury Health Clinic and ask to speak to her."

"What will you tell her?"

"I'll have to figure that out. First, a little search on the Web to see what else we can find out about her."

"This is a wild goose chase."

"You have a better idea?"

The two knew the chance this nurse had the thumb drive was wishful thinking. But what else did they have? Finally, Eduardo smiled, "Great idea. We'll say she must know where it is, and we can make her tell us. I love making a woman talk," he said with a malicious smile. "Even if she doesn't know where it is, I can have some fun."

***

Setting her sail to take better advantage of the wind, Aleandra Lawson, Alex to her friends, the person whose full name was on the card, was taking advantage of Lake Michigan to enjoy a late August Saturday afternoon sail in her thirty-foot sailboat, La Barca de la Señora. She had purchased the boat shortly after moving to Rabbit Island from Cobury, Maryland, to be the nurse practitioner at the Rabbit Island Health Clinic.

Today's wind was from the west, as it was so often on Rabbit Island. Blowing at ten miles an hour with just a few clouds in the sky, it was perfect for a leisurely sail. Alex looked at the telltales, or strings on each side of the jenny, to see if they were parallel, indicating that the boat was getting the most out of the wind. Satisfied, she thought about how lucky she was that the original owner had designed the boat to be sailed by one person.

On her first visit to Rabbit Island, she had been told that the island received its name from early sailors, who, after circumnavigating it, decided its shape resembled a rabbit. Due to a geologic anomaly not yet explained by geologists, the island sits over a volcanic hot spot, making the climate and water around the island warmer than expected by its location near the forty-fifth parallel. Because of the hot spot, the island cools more slowly than the Wisconsin or Michigan shore and has a longer growing season than either mainland. Climate and geography have made it excellent for fruit farming, especially grapes.

Alex reminisced about her rocky start at the Rabbit Island Clinic with the island doctor, Dr. Gould, who had wanted another physician instead of a nurse practitioner. Almost half a year later, he had learned to trust her, and they were working well together. She liked her job, but like all jobs, there were days when, despite her desire to provide the best possible patient care, her hunches were not always correct.

After glancing at the sails to be sure she was still getting the most from La Barca, her thoughts turned to a situation still troubling her. Two weeks ago, when Emma Cobin, an underweight woman in her early sixties, presented to the Clinic with acute pneumonia, Alex had told her she needed to go to Crescent City General. She refused and, in a booming voice, told her, "No, the hospital is where people go to die. If I go, I know I will die."

Alex had countered by saying, "Rabbit Island residents go there all the time and return healthier than when they went. I believe you need the care they can provide."

"No, I'm not going to the hospital, and you can't make me!" Mrs. Cobin had declared emphatically. Twenty years ago, when my mother had pneumonia, they sent her there, and she died."

Before Alex could reply, Dr. Gould, who had heard this exchange, opened the door to the exam room and said, "Dr. Lawson, may I see you outside?"

She hoped he would back her up and tell Mrs. Cobin she needed to go to Crescent City General. Instead, once outside with the door to the room closed, he told Alex, "You can't send her to the hospital. She WILL die there because she believes she will."

"But doctor…"

"We don't need to discuss it. Put together a course of treatment she can do at home. Her daughter is with her and is very capable."

Alex was surprised to hear this. She could not help but remember the young boy whom Dr. Gould had refused to send to Crescent City General despite her firm belief that he had acute appendicitis. Proven right, she had had to make an emergency trip with him and his mother early on a Sunday morning. The surgeon, Dr. Grant, in front of the families of other patients, had yelled at her for waiting until the last minute to send the boy to the hospital and accused her of malpractice. Fortunately, when Dr. Grant called Dr. Gould to complain about her, Dr. Gould told him that he was the one who stopped Alex from sending the boy two days earlier. At that time, Dr. Gould told her that when she disagreed with him, she should state her case and stand by her opinion.

Besides being upset that he forgot this, every sense in her body disagreed. She remembered how Cathy Benton, the Vice President for Nursing at Crescent City General, had told her that Dr. Gould did not send patients to them until they were very sick. As a result, she had replied to the doctor more sarcastically than she intended, "When do you plan to hospitalize her? After she's beyond hope?"

"Dr. Lawson, I have known Mrs. Cobin as a patient since I moved here. She is a strong and, as you found out, stubborn woman. I have found that these long-time island residents are different breeds. They often do better at home than going to the hospital against their will. Discovering that took me a year, but the lesson stayed with me. Send her home with the necessary information and prescriptions. Tomorrow, I will check on her at home. I'm sure that she will be ok. You can visit in a couple of days. Now get started."

Reluctantly, Alex had done as asked. She had been sure that the next day, they were going to have a very sick lady, or worse, but had said nothing more. When the doctor asked her to visit Mrs. Cobin a few days later, she found the lady much improved. Yesterday, Mrs. Cobin returned to the Clinic after recovering from her pneumonia. Seeing Alex, she said, "You see, I didn't need to go to the hospital, did I?"

"No, but I think this time you were lucky. Your daughter took excellent care of you."

"You nurses. Always think hospitals cure everything. They don't."

A wind shift caught Alex's attention. She checked her position and decided to reverse course and return home.. There was a slight possibility of a storm, and Alex did not want to be caught in one. This summer, she learned that they come up out of nowhere near Rabbit Island. The air felt heavy, as it did when one was in the offing. Releasing the jenny, she turned the boat and ducked the boom as it swung to the other side, then pulled in the jenny and set her course for the private channel that led to her dock, sure she would be home before the storm materialized.

Happy with how the boat was sailing, she thought again about Mrs. Cobin. The situation had been a blow to her self-confidence. She had learned earlier that there was always a need to present a confident face to patients. Still, self-doubt was an integral part of practicing in a healthcare profession. She wondered if her success with the acute appendicitis young man had perhaps made her too sure of herself. How far should she go in trying to persuade patients to follow a given course of treatment when they resisted? There is, she realized, no good answer to this. There can be consequences for ignoring medically sound treatment, but, as this case demonstrated, patients have the right to choose their treatment or lack thereof, and they are not always wrong. She concluded that she should chalk this to a learning experience, but not necessarily a hard rule.

Putting that incident out of her mind, she thought about the events a little more than five months ago that led her to Rabbit Island. When budget cuts were made, she was laid off as a nurse practitioner with the Cobury Maryland Clinic because she had the lowest seniority. It was an incidental meeting with Miss Maggie, the island matriarch, during a flight from Honolulu to Chicago that led Alex to move to Rabbit Island. Alex had been instrumental in getting the plane to divert to San Francisco to remove Miss Maggie's great-niece, who had an obstetrical emergency, saving Miss Maggie's great-great-nephew's life and possibly also the great-niece's life.

While the plane was on the ground in Chicago, her seatmate deplaned and did not return. She did not think too much about it until a few months later when FBI agents asked her to identify a murdered man because a business card with her name had been found near his body. She did not know his name but was sure the body belonged to the missing passenger. Unbeknownst to her, the unidentified man, Marco Moretti, had been an accountant with a cartel. Fearing being followed, he placed a thumb drive with incriminating information in Alex's computer case in a small pocket. Since then, several times while talking on the phone, she had absent-mindedly removed the drive and replaced it in the same pocket in her computer case. She had never remembered it long enough to be curious about its contents.

When Marco placed it there, he correctly reasoned she would not find it. When he was murdered, the business card he had taken from her computer case to allow him to find her later had fallen out of his pocket. Two cartel enforcers, Eduardo and Federico, when trying to capture Marco and retrieve the drive, had accidentally killed him but left Alex's business card lying on the ground near Marco.

Had the conversation between Federico and Eduardo about finding her and making her talk been known to Alex, she might not have been so calm. The past few months on Rabbit Island had been a lot of things, mostly positive but never dull. Unexpected, yes. The most unexpected thing was her relationship with Captain Alexander Hamilton, Tony, to her. He was a retired Worldwide Airways Captain, the new owner of Rabbit Island Air, and manager of the commercial side of Rabbit Island Airport. She remembered their first meeting during the obstetrical emergency on the flight from Honolulu to Chicago. They had clashed when he, the captain of the flight, along with a cardiologist and senior flight attendant, did not agree with her diagnosis of a seven-month pregnant woman as having a concealed placental abruption. Luckily, after a phone call to a board-certified obstetrician, who happened to be the wife of the copilot, Captain Hamilton, against the cardiologist's advice, agreed to divert to San Francisco.

Ordinarily, on this sail, Tony would have been with her, but today, he was flying a charter in the two-engine, eight-seater plane that could be converted to an ambulance plane. After he delivered his passengers to Dubuque, Iowa, he planned to spend the day there so he could bring them back. Although Alex and Tony were not technically living together, when he did not have an early morning flight, he usually spent the night at her house.

Charters from Rabbit Island Air, regular commercial service from Blue Water Air, and an undersea fiber-optic cable from Crescent City, Michigan, had attracted new residents who could work from home, but occasionally needed to go into their office. Many of these were previous tourists. Today's client was one of them.

Besides air travel and private boats, transportation to the island was provided by ferry, The Island *Queen*, which transported passengers, freight, and vehicles of all sizes, weather permitting, ran all year. In the summer, the hydrofoil, The *Golden Hind*, added a more frequent and much faster water ferry service for inhabitants and tourists and encouraged day-trippers.

Alex hoped that this afternoon there had been no medical emergencies that required the ambulance plane, but knew that Tony's administrator and pilot, Gina Wistel, plus Bill Yazzie, the pilot from Alaska that Tony had hired as the business expanded, could handle any that happened. Hoping she had not jinxed herself, she heard her phone ring. Seeing the caller ID identifying the caller as Tony, she answered, "Hi, honey."

"I assume you are taking advantage of the beautiful weather and are sailing?"

"Yes, but I miss you. Do you plan to stay here tonight?"

"Yes, assuming I don't get held up by that line of thunderstorms."

"When do you think you'll get here?"

"I was hoping we could leave here about three, but his meetings are lasting longer than he had planned, and his family is enjoying time with old friends. He pays well, so I guess I should not complain. Anyway, fix yourself something to eat, and I'll get something before we leave, by six, I hope."

"Take care and have a safe flight." Studying the sails as she disconnected, she found that under the lee of Rabbit Island, the wind was fluky, causing her to take the sails down and head directly for the channel from the Lake to her dock in front of her house. After safely securing her boat at her dock, she fixed herself a meal from leftovers and settled down for the evening with a book. She was glad that there had been no storm, and she hoped that none had delayed Tony.

At about nine-thirty, Tony walked in. "Made it," he said, pulling her up and giving her a hug and kiss. "The thunderstorms obliged and moved north."

"Do you want anything to eat?"

"I got something before we left Dubuque. I'm tired. Let's go to bed. Maybe tomorrow I can give you another lesson in the two-engine plane."

"Is that a promise?"

"If I get some sleep," he said with a smile as they started for the bedroom.

2 THE CONCERT

Sunday morning was a perfect day for flying. After taking off in the multi-engine eight-seater, Tony turned control over to Alex. He had confidence in her flying abilities and found she quickly adjusted to how the two-engine, larger plane responded to commands.

"It's a little different than the Cessna, but I think I'm getting the hang of it," she said as they enjoyed the flight.

"I believe you are. Let's fly over to Grand Traverse Bay, then Sleeping Bear Dunes. Use the GPS to set your course."

Alex did as instructed, turned, and mischievously asked, "See any boxes down there with antennas?" She was referring to their experiences this past summer when they became involved in stopping a drug cartel from sneaking drugs into the States by dropping a box containing drugs from a passing freighter, which, several hours or even a day later, were located by compatriots using an old-fashioned navigation device, a radio direction finder.

"If I do, we'll ignore them. We don't need any more of that." Looking at the instruments, he told Alex, "You seem to be making many adjustments to keep the plane level. Did you change the gas tanks?"

Chagrinned, Alex looked at the fuel gauges and said, "I'm doing it now." Alex knew when the tank on one side started going down, that side became lighter, making it harder to keep the plane level. She chastised herself for making such a beginner's error. From then on, she paid strict attention to what the airplane and instruments told her.

At the end of their flight, as they were nearing the Rabbit Island Airport, Tony said, "Decent job. You seem to have good instincts. Do you want to land her?"

"Not today. Next time, when I'm rested, I can try it."

"Good idea. Then we'll do some touch-and-goes, or landings and take-offs. But you did well today. There was only one booboo, and I suspect you would have caught that very shortly."

Tony was like her father, a retired pilot for Worldwide Airways. He was a good teacher, but also a perfectionist. Even small praise from him was valuable.

After landing, Alex suggested, "How about a glass of wine at home, then dinner at the Busted Jib?"

"Sounds like a good way to end the weekend."

Over dinner, Tony told her, "Remember that course in airport management in Minneapolis that I told you about. I forgot to tell you last night but I got approval to attend. I will leave here early tomorrow and return on the last Blue Water Air flight Thursday evening. I think I'm doing ok, but I'm sure there are things that I can learn. This means I'll have to get up early. Would you rather I go back to my apartment? I hate to wake you that early."

"I'd rather have you here. Tomorrow should not be too stressful at the Clinic. So, please stay."

"As long as it's ok with you."

"I will miss you while you're gone, but I'm glad for you. As we both know, one can never stop learning. When you gave me lessons so I could renew my pilot's license, I learned quite a few things that I did not know before. Don't tell my dad!"

"Which is why I'm going to the conference, to learn some new things. And there are some sessions aimed at small airports like ours."

"Have a good time too!"

"I wish you were going with me. Minneapolis can be a fun city."

"Maybe next time."

After learning that Tony would be gone until Thursday evening, Miss Maggie called Alex Monday morning and asked her to dinner, saying she had some information to share. Arriving at Miss Maggie's house late after a busier day than planned, she found that Miss Maggie had anticipated that she would probably be stressed and had a Vodka tonic ready for her when she walked in.

"Rough day today?" Miss Maggie inquired.

"Yes, a young child of one of our marine tourists, or those who stay at Nelson's Marina, fell into the lake. It was several minutes before she was found. Fortunately, the staff at Nelson's knew what to do in that situation and were able to locate her quickly. There were no permanent ill effects, but it was tense for a while. I had Rabbit Island Air on alert, but fortunately, they were not needed."

"I heard about that. Thought you would need the drink."

"So true. One never shakes until the crisis is all over."

"I saw the chopper head for Crescent City. But you said you didn't take the little girl to the hospital."

"No, we didn't. However, we transported a tourist staying on a sailboat at Nelson's Marina who broke her arm and needed an open reduction. Gina was able to fly the lady and her husband there."

"Which arm?"

Taking a sip of her drink, Alex said, "The right one, of course, and she is right-handed. She works from home and needs to type. I suggested that she invest in a program that would allow her to dictate and spend the time learning to use it. Even after we gave her some morphine, she was pretty uncomfortable. Once we gave her the morphine, Gina did not want to take her without a nurse aboard. So, I had a round trip to Crescent City. And I still had to see the rest of my patients. Just before I left the Clinic, Cathy Benton, the Vice President for Nursing, called, 'The open reduction on the lady you sent us went well, but there may be some nerve damage.' That was a downer."

"You need to relax. Let's go out to the porch and watch the sunset. It's a little cloudy, and I think it will be colorful."

After settling on the porch, Alex sat her drink down and took a piece of raw broccoli from the vegetable tray that Minnie, Miss Maggie's friend and housekeeper, had thoughtfully provided. She dipped the broccoli into the dip, ate it, sat back, sighed, took a deep breath, and took another sip of her drink.

"I wanted to update you on the plans for the concert this coming weekend to finance our move to electronic health records (EHRs)." Miss Maggie said. "As you know, we are using the natural amphitheater in the Rabbit Island State Park, and both Tony and Chuck Hooper, the owner of Rabbit Island Marine Transport and the *MV Queen* and hydrofoil, the *Golden Hind*, have agreed to a reduced round-trip fare for those with tickets for the concert.

As you know, Brittany Prince, the country singer star, has agreed to do a concert both in the afternoon and evening. Many food vendors from Michigan will feed the concertgoers who don't have time for a restaurant or don't want to spend the money. They all have Department of Health certificates, and I have found locations for them near the beach. Jerry Sutton says he will provide transportation for ticket holders to the concert in one of his large golf carts. How are your plans for the first-aid tent coming?"

"Ann Hooper and I have finalized the arrangements. We will set up the tent the morning of the concert. Jerry has also agreed to bring anyone needing first aid to our tent."

"I'm so pleased. The island is coming together on this. The only remaining item is the weather. The Weather Channel tells me that Saturday we should have a nice day," Miss Maggie said with her usual optimism. "I am told the tickets are almost gone. Chuck has the *Queen*, and the *Golden Hind* almost fully booked for the weekend, even for that last extra run of the *Golden Hind*. Discounts always bring folks in. And the hotels are full."

"I'll bet Nelson's Marina and the smaller one at Steve's Resort are full, too. Tony tells me the Blue Water Air flights are full, and all Jerry's cars are rented. I think this will be a financial success, and we can finally join the rest of the healthcare world with a full-blown electronic health record."

"Sounds like it's all coming together."

Early Friday afternoon, Brittany Prince arrived in her private plane and was given an official greeting by Jeff Peterson, Council President, along with cheers from many fans. Julie and Steve Goodson, the owners of Steve's Island Resort, met her and took her to the hotel, where she is their guest. Her plane then proceeded to the Rabbit Island Air Transport hangar, where the equipment needed for the concert was unloaded and taken to the amphitheater.

Saturday arrived with the promise of sunny weather, temperatures in the mid-seventies, and low humidity. That morning, Alex and Ann worked with the island volunteers to finish setting up the first aid station and get ready for what they hoped would be a low-volume business. Tony had reserved the helicopter and a pilot for the day for any emergency medical transportation and, like Alex and Ann, hoped it would not be needed.

Somehow, perhaps driven by Miss Maggie's thorough planning and the efforts of both long-time and new residents, everything worked out as planned, and the two concerts occurred without a hitch. Although as the first concert was beginning, a storm was seen west of the island, and as Plan B, to protect the performers and their gear, was about to start, the storm had second thoughts and veered north, ignoring the island. Even Police Chief Irving Pauls and an undisclosed number of security personnel, both uniformed and in regular clothes, were surprised.

After the concertgoers from the last concert had left, as Alex and Ann were closing the first-aid tent, Ann commented, "I think we pulled this off, don't you?"

Chuckling, Alex replied. "Although when that storm dared to threaten us, I began to wonder."

Smiling broadly, Ann asked semi-seriously, "Do you think Miss Maggie scared it off?"

Laughing, Alex commented, "Probably. One does not take on Miss Maggie lightly. The storm looked around. Then, not daring to incur her wrath, ignored us."

Later that evening, after the last day trippers and temporary tourists had gone or were settled for the night, Alex and Tony joined many committee members at Miss Maggie's for a celebratory dinner. "This was a tremendous success," Miss Maggie announced. "We've made $25,000. That should ensure we can do a bang-up job of getting started with our EHRs."

"Not bad for a small island located in the middle of Lake Michigan that is only sixteen miles from north to south and twelve from east to west," Ann Hooper said.

"Agreed," came a chorus

Hearing Miss Maggie use the acronym EHR amused Alex. For most of the preceding month, she had referred to them as electronic health records. The thought that she would soon be able to transfer patients more efficiently and enjoy the efficiencies of an EHR was welcome to Alex. She was happy that Miss Maggie had heard her about the need for a full EHR and had put her weight behind it. But, as Alex knew, the success of an EHR depends on usability. She had already contacted IT departments at Crescent City General and Downstate and hoped they understood the importance of usability.

3 MARTA

Monday morning, two weeks after the concert, as Alex, happy that the Clinic would soon have a full EHR, walked into the Clinic, Nora looked up. "The police chief's wife, Mrs. Pauls, Camille, would like you to stop over at the high school this afternoon about three thirty."

"Did she say why?"

"No, just that she needed to ask you something."

At three fifteen, Alex left the Clinic and walked to the high school, avoiding the student traffic, which would have slowed her down. Entering the school, she asked the office where Mrs. Pauls' room was, located it, and walked in through the open door.

Ushering the last student out of her room, Camille saw Alex and said, "I'm glad you could come."

"What's on your mind?"

"Sit down. This may take a while."

With a puzzled look, Alex sat down and waited as Camille moved to a chair near her, sat down, and asked, "Do you know the Novik Family?"

"The family is not one of our regular patients, but I have seen Marta. She's just sixteen, isn't she? She came in with her mother about a month ago, had a bad cut on her lower arm that required several stitches. Said she got it falling."

"Have you seen her for other cuts or bruises?"

"No. Why?"

"Did you ever think the cut could have been part of a pattern of self-mutilation?"

"It never occurred to me. I did, however, notice that she is extremely thin. I mentioned that to her and asked if she would like some help with nutrition. She said 'No,' and I let it go. You can't force people to do things, even when you believe their present actions are hurting them. With a little more weight, she could be very attractive with those dark eyes and dark hair. Except for being too thin, she has a 'well-developed adolescent female body.' Why do you ask?"

"A few days ago, I found her sobbing in the girls' room. I asked her what was wrong, and she said she couldn't tell me. I told her I understood, and she could trust me if she wanted to talk to someone."

"It's frustrating when you want to help but can't, isn't it?"

"There's more. The gym teacher told me that Marta refuses to wear a gym suit, insisting she can play games or exercise just as easily in what she has on as in gym clothes. And she always dresses very modestly. Even on the few days when the temperature is in the high 80s, she comes to school dressed in long sleeves and long pants. And, in an unguarded moment, when she was taking a test, I saw burn marks on her hands and wrists."

"Does not sound good." Pausing, Alex looked at Camille. "You're thinking self-mutilation?"

Camille nodded and said, "The symptoms point to it." She paused, looked out the window, then turned back to Alex and continued, "I'm not sure what we should or can do. She's a loner. All the teachers have noticed she is quiet and has no real friends. The family is first-generation immigrants. Her father works for Vince LeSaul, who bought the winery from Miss Maggie. Her mother works in housekeeping at the Lakeside Inn, which is on the cove just beyond the harbor."

She paused, looking concerned, and quietly added, "The parents are very protective of Marta. She has a younger sister, who is twelve, who is also quiet but does her work. Like Marta, the faculty doesn't believe she is living up to her full potential. The family never comes to school for conferences. And discourage outside relationships. They won't let either girl participate in any after-school activities. In gym class, Marta has shown she's a good softball player. The other girls would love her on their team, but the parents won't give permission. I told Irv about our suspicions, but he said he could do nothing. Told me the police have never had any trouble with the family. They live up on the Highland Road."

Sighing, Alex said, "Unless she comes to the Clinic again, I don't know what I can do."

"If she does, can you try to get her alone and talk with her?"

Alex shifted in her chair, "When a family is controlling and is afraid of outside interference, when we see them there is usually someone who won't leave them alone. But if I get the chance, I'll try."

"Will you let me know if you find anything?"

"Of course. Meanwhile, keep your eyes open and see if you or the gym teacher can establish a rapport with her. I'll see if I can get you some references about self-mutilation."

"We're already on it. Both of us have read what we can find. Marta fits several categories for self-mutilation: she's sixteen, an adolescent female, has low self-esteem, and does not work up to her potential."

"All signs of self-mutilation including the thinness. I'll also talk with Dr. Gould," Alex said, getting up to leave.

"Thanks, Alex. I know you can't just barge in and talk with her, nor can I. Wish I could, though," Camille said wistfully.

"I'm glad you told me. Let's hope we can help her," Alex

said as she left Camille's classroom.

Very early the next morning, Alex's phone rang. She groggily reached for the phone and looked at the clock, which read two AM. Afraid that this was an emergency medical problem, she said in a sleepy voice, "Good morning, or is it still good night?"

"Alex, this is Camille. I hate to bother you at this hour, but it's Marta. About twenty minutes ago she rang our doorbell, crying and telling me she had run away from home because of some man. Can you come over now? I'll send Irv to get you."

"Give me fifteen minutes to get dressed."

Awakened by the call, Tony asked, "Will I need to get up to do an air evacuation?"

"No. Remember last night I told you that Camille told me about a young girl who she believes is self-mutilating. That young girl, Marta, is now at the Pauls. Irv is picking me up. Hope you can get back to sleep."

A short while later, the Police Chief Pauls led Alex into his house. "They're in the guest room," he said leading the way.

Entering the room, Alex saw Marta in the fetal position on the bed with a tissue in her hand, staring into space.

Camille said, "Marta, this is Dr. Lawson. I think you met her once at the Clinic. She can help you if you will let her."

Wiping her eyes with the tissue, Marta closed her eyes and sighed, "No one can help me. Worthless and don't deserve to live."

Alex walked over to Marta, knelt, and put a hand on her shoulder. "Marta, I don't believe that for a minute. We can help you if you let us. I think that by coming here, you are saying you believe we can help."

Marta briefly looked at Alex, turned away, and mumbled, "Tha man won leve me lone. Makes me be bad."

Turning Marta's head so she was facing her, Alex said, "Marta, open your eyes. Did you say a man won't leave you alone?"

Sobbing, Marta shook her head in the affirmative. "Noone bele me," she mumbled and turned away again.

Alex put her arm on Marta's shoulder and said, "Marta, look at me." Marta reluctantly turned her face to look at Alex. "Marta, I believe you, Mrs. Pauls believes you, and Chief Pauls believes you.

"I bad, no good."

"Can you share with us why you think you're bad?"

Pointing at Chief Pauls, Marta said, "No. Him here."

Taking the hint, Irv left the room.

"He's gone now, tell me."

"Is my fath fri. . ."

"Marta, I need you to speak more clearly."

Marta hardened her eyes and threw her arms about as if wiping someone away, "That man! My father's friend won't leave me alone. He...," she stopped and turned away.

"I can see you're angry. If he is doing bad things to you that does not mean you're bad."

Turning her face to Alex, she continued, "Father makes me go for ride with him. He parks in the woods and hurts me down there," she pointed to her groin. "Tells me I have to learn how to be a woman, and he needs to teach me. If I yell, he spanks me hard and hurts me again. I wish I were dead."

"How often does this happen?

"Every time he comes to visit—he came this afternoon and tonight. They make me go with him." Marta started sobbing again as her whole body shook.

Alex pulled her closer, let her cry, and handed her a tissue. "Have you told your parents?"

Between sobs, she blurted out, "I tried to tell," shakes, then adds, "my mother."

"And?" Alex said, waiting patiently for her to continue.

Wiping her face with her tissue, Marta said heatedly, "Tells me stop making up such stories. Says I'm letting my imagination run wild, that I read too much junk. Then sends me to my room until I say I made it all up. Says I'm nothing but a big liar. Then, after dinner tonight – he makes me be bad."

"Marta, he is making himself bad not you. Did you shower before you went to bed?"

"What difference does that make?" Suddenly sitting up, Marta said, "I have to go home. If my father finds out I'm not in the house, he'll whip me. Accuse me of being out with some boy."

"Marta, no one is going to whip you. And because you did not shower, we can make your mother believe you."

"How?"

"I have a friend in Crescent City, June Westen, who is a nurse who works with young women like yourself who have been abused. She can help you prove your story."

"What do I have to do?"

"Let me call her and have her come to the Island. Then come to the Clinic with me."

"Marta, you can stay here until then," Camille said.

"What will she do to me?"

Alex was afraid that telling her that an internal exam would be necessary would make her refuse, but she knew she had to. Slowly, thinking as she talked, she said, "She will examine you internally."

"You mean, down there.," Marta said, pointing with a look of fear.

Calmly, Alex told her, "Yes. But Mrs. Pauls and I will be there with you, and this nurse, a woman, will be very gentle, not like what that man does. When he assaults you, he leaves a liquid in you, which she will collect. It can be analyzed to see if it matches that of the man who is assaulting you."

Marta looked at the floor, trying hard not to start crying again. "Ugh, I don't want his stuff in me. Get it all out. I hate him."

Alex put a gentle hand on Marta's shoulder. "I understand your feelings. I promise you, this will not be anything like what you have already been through. And it will ensure that this will not happen again."

Marta sat quietly for a while and then hesitantly added, "Then he won't be able to do it to my twelve-year-old sister, will he?"

"No."

"My parents will still blame me. Say I encourage him. I hear them talk. Woman is always to blame. That's why they won't let me be away from home except for school." After silence, she added, "But I can save my sister."

"Yes, it will protect your sister, and we will work with your parents to see that they understand."

"I have to go home before I'm missed and get ready for school. What time is it?"

"About 4:00 AM, but you don't need to go to school this morning. This is far more important. And you can stay here with us until we take you to the Clinic," Camille told her.

"But when I'm missed at home, what will happen?"

"What do you think will happen?"

"My father will find me and take me home. Then he will whip me with his belt and tell me he needs to get the bad out of me."

"Marta, that is not going to happen. My husband, Chief Pauls, will take care of anything if it becomes necessary. You are safe now, and we will see you stay safe. You won't need to go home."

Marta looked at Camille and Alex. "But he says, 'The Father will decide how to raise his daughter.'"

"In this country child abuse, which is what whipping with a belt is, is illegal. He can be arrested if he does it," then she added slowly and distinctly, "And you do not have to go home. We will keep you safe,"

Marta looked a little hopeful. She looked at Alex and said, "I will go to the Clinic. Are you sure you can keep me safe?"

"I am sure," Camille told her followed by Alex repeating the information.

4 JUNE WESTIN

Having told Marta Novic that she would call her friend June Westen, the sexual assault nurse examiner in Crescent City, Alex left Marta with Camille. She hoped June would be available. She knew she had stretched things when she said June was her friend. She had just met her once when she was with Cathy Benton at Crescent City General, and hoped she would remember that she had offered her services to Rabbit Island if needed. But she did not know how to contact her. Cathy would know, but at this hour, Cathy would not be home, and she did not have her cell number.

Seeing Irv, Alex asked, "Can you get a home phone number for Cathy Benton at Crescent City General so I can contact June Westen, the sexual assault nurse examiner at Crescent City General?"

"I can do better than that. I can get June's number." Within a few minutes, Irv handed Alex a piece of paper, saying, "This is June's cell number."

When June answered the phone, Alex said, "This is Alex Lawson from Rabbit Island. I'm sorry to call you this early, but I have a problem.

"In this field 24-hour call is part of the job. What's your problem?"

Alex then related what Marta had told her and asked,

"Can you come over to Rabbit Island this morning?"

"I can catch the first ferry at quarter to eight this morning."

"Forget that. How soon can you be at the Crescent City General heliport? We'll have someone pick you up there."

"Let's see, it's now about quarter to five. I could be there by six."

"Ok, unless you hear from me, someone will meet you and bring you here."

The call concluded, Alex called Tony and told him what she had promised, asking if it was possible.

"I can do it," he said. "Will you be with me?"

"Not this time. Bring June to the Clinic and tell her I will meet her there. I'll tell you all about it later."

Glad that June was available, and that Tony could pick her up, Alex returned to Camille and Marta. Marta had fallen into a restless sleep and Alex quietly told Camille what they had arranged, saying, "They should be at the Clinic about six thirty. About six fifteen, we will wake Marta and take her to the Clinic."

Camille and Alex had just settled Marta in a room in the Clinic when they heard the whap, whap of the helicopter as it descended to the roof. "I'll go meet her," Alex told them. As June exited the helicopter Alex said, "Thank you for coming so quickly."

"I'm used to this. Life in this business is always an emergency," June replied following Alec down the stairs to the Clinic as Alex filled her in on the situation. "It's good she has not showered," June said. "I believe we can get some evidence of who did this to her. But we will need DNA from the assumed perp."

"Chief Pauls said he would work on that. Marta said his name is Cedric X. Smith, and he lives in Columbus, OH. With luck, they have his DNA on file."

"Good luck with that. I doubt he will give it voluntarily," June said as they entered Marta and Camille's room.

"Marta, this is the nurse I told you about, June Westen. She specializes in helping young ladies like you."

With a gentle voice, June approached Marta, gently touched her shoulder, and, looking into her eyes, said, "Marta, I'm sorry about what has happened to you, and I want to make sure that it never happens again."

Marta studied June but said nothing.

"To do this, I will need to examine you internally and take some samples. With that sample, we can get evidence of who your assailant is."

With a blank expression, Marta said quietly, "Okay, . . . I guess."

June was good at her job, and the exam was done quickly. June kept up encouraging remarks to Marta, and Camille and Alex supported Marta.

"All over, Marta. You were very helpful," June said. Turning away from Marta, June said, "Alex, why don't you and Camille leave us alone now?" After they left, she returned to Marta. "I am concerned about some of the cuts and scars I see on your legs. How did they happen? You can tell me. I won't tell anyone.

Her face a wooden mask, Marta said, "I'm bad, have to punish myself."

"Marta, why don't you sit up and get dressed while I find a more comfortable place for you and me to talk."

"Just you?"

"Yes, this is between just you and me." Opening the door June asked Alex, "Is there a room where Marta and I can talk?"

"I think you can use the conference room. I'll check to see that it is not scheduled this morning. Would either of you like a cup of coffee?"

"I would love one," June said. "Black, how about you, Marta?"

"I don't drink coffee. Do you have any juice?"

"I think I can find some orange juice, is that ok?" Alex answered.

Marta nodded her head in the affirmative.

"I'll bring coffee and juice to the conference room. As soon as you're ready, I'll take you both there. It will be at least an hour before Nora or the doctor gets here, so take your time."

As the coffee was being made, Alex guided June and Marta to the conference room, where she had thoughtfully placed a box of tissues. "I'll be right back with the coffee and juice," she told them.

After delivering the beverages, Alex closed the door to the conference room, saying that no one would be coming in but to call if they needed anything.

Her job temporarily done, Alex poured herself a cup of coffee and added some cream and sugar. A box of Friday's donuts had one left, albeit stale, but Alex ate it anyway, discovering that she was hungry. If she had her car she would have gone to the Busted Jib, but she did not feel like an early morning walk. Just then, she heard a knock on the Clinic door. She went to the waiting room and saw Tony with a bag at the door.

She let him in as he smiled and said, "I thought you might be hungry. Josie sent you some eggs, bacon, and one of the English muffins she knows you like."

"Thanks. You must be a mind reader. I was just wishing I could go to the Busted Jib, and you brought it to me."

"We can go to your office and enjoy a little breakfast."

"Tony, I think we should stay here. I can clear this table, get us some coffee, and we can eat here. June is with the patient in the conference room, and I don't want the patient hearing anyone outside the door."

Alex left to get the coffee while Tony cleared a space for them to eat. As Alex returned to the waiting room, Tony said, "I'm guessing you have already had a stressful day."

"You made it less stressful by getting June here."

"Who is she?"

Alex explained who June was and said there was a case of sexual assault."

"And patient privacy keeps the rest confidential, right?" Tony commented.

As they were finishing their breakfast, June called, and Alex went back to the conference room to see what she needed. "Alex, we're going to have a family problem. Marta does not want to go home, and I don't want her to. I don't think that, at present, it's safe. She's sixteen and can legally be declared an emancipated adult, but we need a court order. Without it, I don't want to take her off the island. I know a lawyer in Crescent City who could arrange this. The difficulty is that I don't want to ruin the family relationship permanently. She will need support, and the family is the best place, but the family needs help to accept the real situation and our culture. From what Marta said, they are in complete denial. And I believe her. I've seen it before. I think they love her, but adjusting to a new culture and not wanting to believe that a supposedly good friend would do this will be a tough sell."

"Understand," Alex replied

"Of course, we'll have to get DNA from the perp."

"As I think I mentioned, Camille's husband, the Chief of Police, is working on that angle."

"If it can be worked out, I would like to take Marta with me to Crescent City and put her in a place where she will be safe and get the care, both physically and mentally, she needs.

I've suggested that to her, and she wants to go with me. If I can use your phone, I will call my lawyer friend. Meanwhile, someone needs to contact her family."

"Use the phone in my office, it's private there. It's the door to the right of the conference room and is open. Meanwhile, I'll contact Chief Pauls and see what he can do about contacting the family. Perhaps he can take Camille with him. Marta is one of her students."

As soon as June went to call the lawyer, Alex called Chief Pauls and relayed what June had told her, asking him if he and Camille could visit the family.

"I was thinking that needed to be done," he replied. "Frankly, I'm surprised no one has shown up at the station to declare her missing. On the bright side, I was able to contact the police in Columbus. We are in luck, a teen-age girl accused Cedric of being the father of her baby, and took a DNA test to prove he was not. They still have his DNA and will send us a sample."

"That is good news."

Alex hung up just as Nora walked in, surprised to see Tony clearing up breakfast remains in the waiting room. "What is happening here?" she asked.

"It's been an interesting morning. We have a sexually assaulted young girl in the conference room with June Westen, who is arranging to take her to safety."

Noticing Tony's presence, Nora acknowledged the information, calmly asking what she could do to help.

"Help us clean up this mess before our first patient arrives," Alex told her.

"No problem."

"Thanks, Nora."

Entering the Clinic waiting room, June announced, I have legal permission to take Marta to Crescent City."

"That's a relief," Alex said.

"What time is it?" June asked.

"About 7:30," Nora replied.

"That's enough time to catch the 9:30 *Golden Hind*," Alex informed them. "And grab a bite to eat at the Busted Jib. My friend, Captain Hamilton, or Tony as we know him, will take you there. I am so glad you were able to come this morning."

"So am I. I'm afraid this is going to be a long case."

5 THE DULIAMIS

A few weeks later, as Alex was walking to her office with a cup of coffee, Nora stopped her in the hall and told her that Mrs. Duliami, Nadia's mother, had come in with a splitting headache. "She's in room three, and I think you need to go there right away. I took her blood pressure, and it was "190 over 130."

"Thanks for seeing us," Nadia greeted her. "My mother has the worst headache she's ever had. Nothing in my experience or my mother's explains this." Mrs. Duliami had been a midwife in Iraq and had been training her daughter to follow in her footsteps when they were able to emigrate to the US. In Iraq, she was more than a midwife, being the only person with medical knowledge for miles around. Nadia had used the knowledge her mother had taught her during the school bus accident the previous year to save the Goodsons' daughter from becoming a quadriplegic, as well as rescuing Noah Foxworthy when he had a chest injury. Alex had not had contact with her since the accident.

Looking at Mrs. Duliami, Alex saw pain etched on her face. "Let's get you on the exam table and as comfortable as possible," she said to the woman. "Nadia, you can help."

Once Mrs. Duliami was on the exam table, Alex could see a drooping eyelid. Reacting to the light in the room, Mrs. Duliami said in a halting voice, "Light, too bright."

Alex immediately turned off the light as the patient

said, "So sleepy, just let me sleep."

"Nadia, what brought this on?"

"I don't know. She was nauseous and vomited last night and during the trip here. And she's been confused. And complained of eye pain."

Alex reviewed in her mind Mrs. Duliami's symptoms: the sudden severe headache, the drooping eyelid, and her reaction to light, all symptoms of a ruptured or leaking cerebral aneurysm. Hoping she was wrong but not wanting to take any chances, Alex said, "Mrs. Duliami, I am very concerned about your condition. I want to airlift you as soon as possible, probably to Downstate Medical Center. I believe you may have a cerebral aneurysm, or a weakened or leaking artery in your brain, and need a neurologist. Nadia, please stay with your mother while I call a neurologist."

"Can't you do something here?"

"Nadia, I'm afraid it's far more serious than what we can do here or at Crescent City General."

Looking concerned, Nadia said, "Do what you think is best."

Alex placed a call to Downstate Medical Center and soon was talking with the chief neurologist.

"We've not treated many of these. Your best bet is Dr. Michael Norse at Northwestern. We send these patients to him."

"Thank you, I know him. I had the privilege of working with him in Iraq. The patients that he cared for were lucky. He did some miraculous work there."

"I believe you. Dr. Larson, hang up and call him."

Answering his phone, Dr. Norse, an African American neurologist at Northwestern Medical Center said, "Colonel Lawson, what an unexpected pleasure. What can I do for you?"

Alex explained the situation, and he replied that she

should get the patient to him as soon as possible. "Can you airlift her immediately?"

"I think so."

"I will put her at the top of my priority list today. Call me when you have an ETA, and I will meet the chopper. Don't fly too high. We don't need oxygen deprivation. And start oxygen on her."

"Thank you. I will be in touch as soon as I know our ETA. And I will do as complete a history as I can. We have never seen the patient before; she was a midwife in Iraq, and she and her daughter settled here on Rabbit Island." Probably arranged by Miss Maggie, Alex thought.

"What's her name? At one of my posts, I worked with an Iraqi midwife."

"Chiva Duliami.

"Duliami, I remember a Chiva Duliami and her daughter. They were the only medical care around, and we would help out with the citizens when we could. When we sent a citizen home earlier than we would have here in the States, we knew Mrs. Duliami and her daughter would care for the patient well. I don't know how they managed, but they did. Isn't her daughter's name Nadia?"

"Yes, and she is with her."

"I'll have a team meet you. When I worked with them, Nadia seemed very bright. By the way, I want you to come with her during the transport; I don't trust anyone else."

"See you shortly."

You're sending a patient to Northwestern?" Dr. Gould, who had learned about the situation, said.

"Yes. Downstate referred us to him. I know the neurologist, and he is the best."

It was Gina who answered when Alex called Rabbit Island Air. "What do you want? Tony's not here."

"I have a patient with a suspected cerebral aneurysm,

possibly already a small leak. We need to get her to Northwestern Medical Center in Chicago ASAP."

"Why not Downstate. That's much closer."

"Because of a neurologist who is familiar with this type of condition."

"I think you should take her to Downstate," Gina replied.

Alex was irritated that Gina thought she could make medical decisions. "I'll let Tony know when I see him, meanwhile I'm busy."

Before Gina could hang up, Alex quickly interrupted, "Gina. this is an emergency, a life-or-death situation. Find Tony NOW and tell him," Alex said, frustrated at Gina's very unprofessional behavior.

"All right, all right, don't get huffy."

"Alex, what do you need?" She was surprised to hear Tony's voice.

Alex repeated her request and told him they needed to take a patient to Northwestern Medical Center in Chicago.

"I will prepare the chopper and be on your roof as soon as possible."

As Alex returned, Nora was bringing a gurney to the exam room. Mrs. Duliami had fallen asleep, and Nadia asked, "Why the gurney?"

"Nadia, we are transporting your mother to Northwestern Medical Center in Chicago.

"My mom has to go to work, and I need to go to school."

"Don't worry, I will notify Steve's Island Resort that their head housekeeper can't make it, as well as your school. Let's get your mother to the roof and all three of us on the chopper."

"But why Chicago, why not Crescent City General or Downstate?" Nadia asked.

There is a neurologist in Chicago who specializes in this

condition. I believe you know him, Dr. Michael Norse."

With relief on her face, Nadia said, "Yes, we know him." Turning to her mother, she said, "Mom, Dr. Norse is going to take care of you." She thought she noted a slight acknowledgement from her mother at the news. While helping to move Mrs. Duliami to the gurney, Nadia said, "I know Dr. Norse will do his best for Mom."

"In about fifteen minutes, we will all go to the heliport on the roof. The chopper will be here in about 20 minutes," Alex told the patient and her daughter. With Mrs. Duliami sleeping, Alex left the room to inform Dr. Gould of what was happening.

"Good call, Dr. Larson," he told her." I only hope we can get her there in time. Besides reading a few of his articles, I had the privilege of hearing Dr. Norse at a conference a few years ago. He is top-notch."

"The neurologist at Downstate referred me to him. And the Duliamis know him, and he knows them. He used to send patients to them when he was in their area in Iraq."

"Even better. Nora and I will take care of your patients this morning. You go with the Duliamis."

"Thanks. I have no idea when I will be back."

"Don't worry, we will manage. Now, get the Duliamis up to the heliport."

Shortly, Alex, the patient, and her daughter were aboard the helicopter and headed for Chicago. As soon as they were safely airborne, Alex called Dr. Norse, giving him their ETA. After the call, Alex checked her patient, adjusted the oxygen and IV, and settled down to watch for any changes.

She was amused to see that Gina had accompanied Tony. She was glad it was not just Gina piloting. She had no desire to be abandoned in Chicago and was afraid Gina might do that.

During the flight, Alex used the rough notes she had

made about the treatment they had provided for Mrs. Duliami, added Nadia's history, and wrote a transfer note.

True to his word, Dr. Norse greeted them at the Northwestern heliport. As they took the patient off the helicopter, he said, "Mrs. Duliami! I'll take good care of you, just as you did the patients we sent you." The patient did not acknowledge the doctor, but Nadia was sure her mother had heard. Turning to Nadia, Dr. Norse put a hand on her shoulder and said in a comforting voice, "Nadia, rest assured, your mother will get the best care we can provide. I'd heard you'd been allowed to come to the States but had no idea where you were."

Nadia had become visibly relaxed at seeing Dr. Norse. "Dr. Norse, I'm so glad you will care for my mother."

"Nadia. I've already called my wife, and she is preparing a room for you to use. You may want to stay at the hospital tonight, but we want you to stay with us while you are here. You will need to get away from the hospital."

Tears in her eyes, Nadia just looked at the doctor. "Thank you," was all she managed to say.

Turning to Alex, Dr. Norse said, "Your mission is done. Go home with the bird, and I will keep you apprised about Mrs. Duliami. You didn't know we were friends, did you?"

"No, but I'm glad it worked out like this."

"At one of my bases in Iraq, I had several occasions to work with both Duliamis. As you may have guessed, Mrs. Duliami was often the only medical person for a hundred miles until we camped there."

"I know what you mean. I saw those situations too."

Smiling, Dr. Norse said, "I'll take good care of your two Rabbit Island Citizens. One of these days, I will have to spend some time on your island."

"We would be delighted," Alex said, waving goodbye and climbing aboard the helicopter for the trip back to Rabbit

Island. She would have liked to share the turn of events with Tony, but she was obviously unwelcome in the vicinity of the pilots. Guess Gina had not forgiven her for being with Tony. Instead, she settled in and took the time to relax and enjoy the ever-changing colors on Lake Michigan.

It was one-thirty before Alex returned to the Clinic. Nora greeted her, saying, "A woman from your old job named Connie called and wants you to call. I guess they want to check up on you."

"Thanks, Nora. If I don't have any patients waiting, I'll call her from my office."

"You are lucky, you are free until about three."

Sitting down in her office, Alex picked up the phone, called her old Clinic, and said, "Hi Connie, what's up?"

"Nothing out of the ordinary. But it's not the same without you. Pam and Ellie said to say 'Hi' to you. The last I heard about you, you and that airplane pilot had just helped to break up a drug ring."

"Thank heavens that's over." Alex paused, "How is everything there? I do like it here, but I miss you all."

"Outside of missing you, it's the same as when you were here."

How about visiting me this summer? Get out of the heat."

"We might surprise you!"

"That would be great."

"To change the subject, do you know a Major Hugo Baxter?"

"No, should I?"

"He called here asking for you. Said he was a former patient."

"I don't remember any Major Baxter, but then I don't remember every patient we cared for. I suppose I could have met him."

"He said he now lives in Salisbury and would like to see you again to thank you. He wanted you to know that he had recovered completely and was sure it was due to your excellent care."

"Nice to hear, but we cared for a lot of patients. I don't recall him."

"I hope you're not upset. I gave him your contact information at the Rabbit Island Clinic. Don't be surprised if he calls."

He did not call that afternoon, and Alex thought he probably had decided that he could not visit her because she was no longer local. She did not know that after the supposed Major discontinued the call with Connie, he turned to his colleague, Eduardo, and said, "That nurse is no longer in Cobury, but I know where she is."

"Where?" Eduardo asked."

On some little island called Rabbit Island in the middle of Lake Michigan. Shouldn't be too hard to find her and get that thumb drive."

"Good work, Federico," his colleague, Eduardo, told him. "Let's tell Javier and say we will find her and the drive. He still thinks that drive exists and is desperate to get his hands on it."

6 ACUTE CHOLECYSTITIS

Not receiving a call from the Major, Alex completely forgot about the call from Connie. The rest of the week at the Rabbit Island Clinic was uneventful except for being very busy. By Thursday, everyone was looking forward to the weekend. After looking at the appointment book for Friday and seeing only two appointments, Dr. Gould asked Nora to move those appointments so they could close the Clinic at noon.

When Alex heard, she asked Dr. Gould. "Are we going to make a habit of closing at noon on Friday?"

"If there are not a lot of patients scheduled in the afternoon, we can, at least in the fall. Nora will have little trouble moving these two. So, make plans if you want. It's supposed to be a beautiful day. I'll stick around in case something comes up and use the time to update some records. By the end of the month, we should be moving to electronic health records (EHRs), and I want to be ready. We'll probably have longer hours until we learn to use it."

"Possibly, but after we become familiar with it, it should make the work faster." As soon as she could, Alex called Tony and told him, "We're closing the Clinic at noon on Friday. Can you free up the afternoon? If you can, we could go sailing."

"I think I can, barring no medical emergencies." In a joking voice, he added, "Preventing medical emergencies is up to you."

"I'll try to make sure no one comes up with one," Alex said, laughing.

"Ok, it's a date!"

Friday noon, as Alex was leaving the Clinic, Nora apologetically stopped her, saying, "I know the Clinic is supposed to close today at noon, but Mrs. Anna Bailey just came in with severe pain, and Dr. Gould is still with another patient. I put her in room three. She's clutching at her abdomen and is sick to her stomach. Amy Shepherd, her neighbor, brought her in and is with her. I think you'll need morphine. I'll bring it to you."

"Thanks. I'll go right in." Taking the record from Nora and glancing at it as she made her way to exam room three. She read, 'Age 63, overweight, a widow, lives near the Shepherd's, had no complaints at her physical exam this past summer.' Outside the door to the exam room, Alex heard moaning. Entering, she saw Mrs. Bailey sitting on a chair. "Mrs. Bailey, I can see you're in pain. Nora is getting a pain reliever. Would you like that before we try to figure out your problem?"

"Oh yes." The woman looked up at Alex, clutching her upper right abdomen, taking quick breaths, her face tight, perspiration on her forehead.

"Can Amy and I help you walk to the exam table?"

"It hurts so much." Mrs. Bailey said, but between the two of them, she made it to the table, where Alex tried to make her as comfortable as possible. As Nora entered the room with the medication, Alex turned to Amy, "Amy, can you stand next to her to be sure she does not fall off the table?"

Amy nodded her assent as Alex said, "Mrs. Bailey, I will fix a pain med shot for you, ok?"

"If it will stop the pain."

"It won't be instantaneous like you see on TV, but it will

not take too long," Alex told her while pulling the medicine into the syringe.

After receiving the injection, Mrs. Bailey said, "I'm so cold."

Alex quickly got a blanket from the warmer and placed it over the patient. As the woman's face started to relax, Alex asked, "Where does it hurt the most?"

Pointing to the area just under her right ribcage, Mrs. Bailey said, "Here, and it seems to also hurt in my upper back."

"When did the pain start?"

"About an hour ago."

Wondering if the symptoms meant a gallbladder attack, Alex asked, "When did you last eat?"

Nodding at Amy, she said, "I had a wonderful brunch with Amy at the Busted Jib."

"Bacon and eggs, yes?"

"And several English muffins," which Alex suspected were heavily buttered. "But I lost it all on the way here. And I feel nauseous now."

Getting an emesis basin from a cupboard, Alex asked, "Tell me, Mrs. Bailey, in the past few weeks or months, have you been troubled with bloating, mild pain, or abdominal discomfort? Particularly after a large meal?"

"I guess so. Come to think of it, always after I have a wonderful meal."

"You didn't mention this when Dr. Gould saw you last summer."

"It didn't seem worthwhile. If I had, it would have meant tests at Crescent City General. I'm healthy, I don't need tests."

"I can understand how you feel. I suspect I don't have to tell you tests are ordered to catch problems before they become emergencies. Were you afraid they would find something?"

"No, just did not want to go to Crescent City General for a day."

"Understandable. Have you ever had your appendix out?"

"Yes, when I was fourteen. So, it can't be appendicitis."

"No, but it's possible that right now you're suffering an acute gall bladder attack. You probably have gallstones, and one or more are trying to pass through your bile duct or the tube from your gall bladder to your intestine, but the duct is blocked. The bile duct continuously creates jerking movements to try and clear the problem, creating your pain."

"What should I do about it?"

"Let me do an ultrasound of your gall bladder, and then we can see what is happening."

"Why can't I just tough it out?"

"You could, but that could be dangerous, and the pain may not stop.. If the blockage is below where the liver empties bile into your small intestine, you could develop an inflammation of your pancreas or develop liver problems. I would not recommend it."

"I'm feeling better now. I need to wait."

"Mrs. Bailey, you're feeling better because of the morphine. If my suspicions are correct, the danger is still there, and the pain will return when the drug wears off. After the ultrasound, we can make a more informed decision."

"If you insist."

The ultrasound confirmed Alex's diagnosis, and she told Mrs. Bailey, "I recommend that I contact Rabbit Island Air, and we get you there as soon as possible."

"Why can't I take the ferry?"

"Because the ferry schedule will get you there too late. The ultrasound suggests that you may need immediate surgery. And they like to close early on Friday, so later is not good."

"I can't have surgery and be hospitalized. My cats need to be fed, and I have nothing with me."

Amy immediately said, "Anna, I will care for your cats. They know me, and I like them. And, if you have to stay at the hospital, I'll also water your plants. I think you should do as Dr. Larson suggests."

"But I can't be away from home for a week. My aunt had gallbladder surgery and was in the hospital for ten days, and was very sick."

"How long ago was that?"

"Probably 40 years, but she talked about the pain and being miserable until her death."

"Mrs. Bailey, things are far better today. Instead of opening the abdomen or belly, most surgery for gallstones is done with what we call laparoscopy, and you are not hospitalized more than overnight. Some patients even go home the same day."

"How do they do that?"

"The surgeon makes a few small incisions and inserts a thin rod with a camera attached, and performs the surgery without disturbing other organs, which is what caused a lot of discomfort back then. During this surgery, you will be under conscious sedation and won't feel a thing. And because they will not open your belly, you will recover quickly."

Mrs. Bailey sighed. "You're not just saying that to get me to go to the hospital, are you?"

"I don't do that. If I lied to you, you would never believe me again, and it would not be good for me or the Clinic. I assure you, what I told you is the truth. If you ignore this, you could end up very sick."

Looking defeated, she replied, "All right, I guess." With a pleading look, she asked Amy. "Will you come with me? Then, if I can come home, you can bring me. If I can't, could your husband, Logan, feed my cats?"

"I think he can and would. I'll call him and ask him."

"Mrs. Bailey, I'm going to call Rabbit Island Air, ok?"

"I guess so. If you think it's absolutely necessary?"

"I do. If it were me, I would be on my way to Crescent City General at this very moment."

After calling Rabbit Island Air, Alex saw Dr. Gould in the hall, "I see you decided to send Anna Bailey to Crescent City General."

"Yes, the chopper will be here in about 15 minutes."

"What do you suspect?"

"The ultrasound confirms a blockage of the bile duct."

"She loves her food, the fattier the better. I asked her about her diet during her summer visit, but did not press it. Patients won't do anything until they're ready. Come to think of it, I noticed then that she was bloated, but she just said it was the beans she had eaten the night before. And added, 'I'm not going to have any tests so they can again tell me I'm too fat.' I hated to hear that she had that opinion of Crescent City General, but she could have run into a less-than-feeling person there who thought that would motivate her. Wrong, of course."

"Thanks, Dr. Gould." Alex could not help but remember that less than four months ago, he would have demanded to examine the patient himself because he did not trust her judgment.

"Let me know how it comes out. Why don't you go with her? I know you were planning to have the afternoon off, but I would be more comfortable if you went with her, and so would she. And while you're at Crescent City General, would you check on Mr. Dneiper? Last week we sent him there with an acute infection. He was on the way to sepsis. Last I knew, he was in a bad way and in the ICU."

Sighing inwardly, knowing this would add at least

fifteen minutes and probably closer to half an hour to the trip, Alex said, "I remember him. I will do that and send you a text when we are on our way back to Rabbit Island."

"Thanks, Alex, I owe you."

Alex left him, retrieved a gurney, and took it to the exam room. Entering the room, she said, The Rabbit Island Air helicopter will be at the Clinic heliport shortly. Meanwhile, we need to get you up there. Amy and I will help you onto this rolling bed." She turned to Amy, "Were you able to reach Logan?"

"Yes, and he will take care of the cats."

By the time they had wheeled Mrs. Bailey to the elevator to the heliport, they could hear the helicopter approaching. To avoid the heavy wind as the chopper descended, they stayed behind the door to the heliport. Gina Wistel helped them load Mrs. Bailey onto the helicopter and secure her. When she knew all the passengers were safely buckled in, she took a seat as the copilot.

A voice from the other side of the cockpit said, "Well, Dr. Larson, I see you couldn't resist a medical emergency this afternoon."

"And hello to you, too, Captain Hamilton," Alex said, smiling. "Now, how about getting this bird to Crescent City General pronto? There will still be some time for a sail after that."

"At your service, Dr.," came the laughing reply. Within fifteen minutes, they landed at Crescent City General, where the ER team, who had been notified, met them.

Surprising Alex, the ER team that met the helicopter from Rabbit Island included Dr. Grant.

"Welcome to Crescent City General, Dr. Lawson. I hope this time you brought us a patient well before the crisis stage." He was referring to their first meeting when he had to come in very early one Sunday morning and do an emergency appendectomy on a patient who should have been referred two days earlier. He had been very upset and had taken it out on Alex, telling her she was incompetent. Fortunately, when he had called Dr. Gould to report her, Dr. Gould had told him that it was he, not Alex, who had prevented the young boy from being sent to the hospital earlier. Chagrined, Dr. Grant had sought Alex out the next time he saw her at the hospital and apologized profusely.

"I'm not that sure we were early enough to avoid a crisis, but this is the first chance we had," Alex said. "Dr. Grant, meet Mrs. Anna Bailey. Mrs. Bailey, this is Dr. Grant." Turning to the doctor, Alex said, "Dr. Grant, I did an ultrasound, and there is a blockage in the bile duct. I sent you the results. She had morphine about twenty-five minutes ago." Alex then briefed Dr. Grant with as much of Mrs. Bailey's medical history as she could remember, adding, "In the not-too-distant future, I hope you will be able to access our patient records. As you know, we are installing electronic records next month."

"That will be welcome," He turned to the team. "Take this patient to preop. After seeing your ultrasound, I booked surgery, even though it's Friday afternoon." Seeing Amy, he asked her, "Will you accompany her to preop?"

"I would like to."

"Then do so. We welcome support people."

"Dr. Grant, this is Amy Shepherd. You may remember her. A few months ago, she was a patient here, after being transferred from Downstate Medical Center, recovering from a gunshot wound."

"Good to see you again and healthy," Dr. Grant told her. "Why don't you follow the gurney? We'll catch up in a minute."

Turning to Alex, he said, "It's good to see you again. I'm glad you didn't hold my obnoxious behavior against me."

"You apologized. It's water under the dam." Handing him a few papers, Alex continued, "Here is the transfer note I wrote on the way over."

Turning to Tony, she said, "Tony, Dr. Gould asked me to check on another patient. It won't take long, will you wait for me?"

"Of course," he answered as he and Gina left to chat with the Crescent City General helicopter pilot.

7 ABANDONMENT

After leaving Tony and asking him to wait while she checked on Mr. Dneiper as Dr. Gould had asked, Alex heard, "Dr. Larson." Turning around, she saw Cathy Benton, the vice president for nursing, approaching. " It seems like a long time since I saw you. How about a cup of coffee before you go back?"

"Cathy, I'd love to, but I told Captain Hamilton to wait for me. And I need to check on a patient, a Mr. Dnieper."

"I'll take you to see Mr. Dneiper. He's on 4 East. We just transferred him out of ICU yesterday."

As they were going to see the patient, Cathy told her, "By the way, the charge nurse on 4 East is certified in med/surg nursing."

"That's great. It's nice that your hospital values its nurses and raises their pay when they get certified in their field. Not that usual for a hospital this size."

"We are very proud of that. It helped us to get our Medicare approval back after our oncology scandal. And I'm sure we will soon have Magnet Hospital accreditation again."

"Dark days, weren't they?"

"And then some. But they are behind us now, and we are doing well building back the community's trust."

"I'm glad to hear it."

Entering the unit and approaching the charge nurse, Cathy asked, "How is Mr. Dneiper today? Dr. Lawson is here to see him."

"As a visitor, not as a nurse practitioner." Alex was quick to add.

"He's doing well. I think he may be able to go back to Rabbit Island before another week is over. We don't want to release him too soon, but many patients get better more quickly at home. And, with you available on the island, I think if he has more problems, which I think is unlikely, he'll be ok; his wife has been staying here with him. He's in room 435. You can go in now if you'd like."

"Thank you," Alex told her. Turning to Cathy, she said, "Thanks for the guide. I'll take a rain check on that coffee."

Entering the patient's room, Alex said, "Good afternoon, Mr. and Mrs. Dneiper. I'm so glad to see you here and not in the ICU."

"We're glad, too," Mrs. Dneiper replied.

After a few minutes of conversation, Alex said, "Remember when you get back to the island, we are only a phone call away. I'm sure you will be ok, but I just wanted to assure you that you won't be alone in the unlikely event you need help."

"Thank you, Dr. Lawson. It will be great to get him home, and I will take great care of him."

"I'm sure you will. Have a good rest of the day."

Returning to the heliport, Alex found the Rabbit Island Air helicopter gone. Wondering if there was another call, Alex asked the Crescent City General pilot, "Where did the Rabbit Island helicopter go? I expected Captain Hamilton to wait for me."

"They said you told a nurse to tell them you would not be coming back for about two hours, and they shouldn't wait for you."

"Who told them that?"

"A nurse in the ER, I think."

Inwardly seething, Alex said, "Thank you for the information," and left to walk to the ferry dock. Now she'd have to wait for the 2:15 *Golden Hind*, which wouldn't get her back to Rabbit Island until 3:30, making for a very short sail. Obviously, Tony didn't want to go sailing this afternoon. Why didn't he say so instead of stranding me?

Usually, Alex enjoyed waiting at the ferry dock watching the other boats in the harbor, but not today. Eventually, she saw the *Golden Hind* enter the harbor and dock. Ignoring the other passengers as she boarded, she sat on the port side, where she had a view of the Lake. Most of the time, she enjoyed the trip on the hydrofoil, but today she was angry. Why would Tony take someone's word that she said not to wait for her? He should have called her and double-checked. Why didn't he? Was he, after all, just another untrustworthy flyboy?

She forced herself to smile as Crystal Foxworthy, another island resident, sat beside her. "Alex, I'm surprised to see you here."

"I helped bring an emergency here, and the helicopter couldn't wait for me."

"I hope whoever it is is ok. I know you can't tell me who."

"I'm pretty sure the person will be ok. What are you doing on the mainland?"

"I needed to buy some things before winter, when the *Queen* can't always make the trip. This will be your first winter on the island, yes?"

"Yes, it will. Miss Maggie told me I must plan and buy as many non-perishables as possible. Mike's General Store stays open, doesn't it?"

"Yes, but they can run short. It pays to be prepared to make a week's worth of meals from what you have. Although I could buy all these things at Mike's, he would be wiped out if I and everyone else bought the quantity we need."

"Sounds like a good idea to go to Crescent City for this. Prices are a little less on the mainland, yes?"

"Yes, stuff doesn't have to be transported as far. Now to catch up on my reading."

As Crystal opened her book, Alex took out her phone and texted Dr. Gould the news about Mr. Dneiper, then sat back and tried to relax, but her anger at being left in Crescent City made it difficult. Excusing herself, she went out on deck to get some air.

In the distance, she saw a sailboat, which reminded her of what she had planned to do that afternoon. As the hydrofoil closed the distance to the sailboat, she studied it. To her, it looked like her boat, La Barca. She didn't know there was another sailboat like hers in the area. She'd have to meet the owners and compare notes.

Twenty minutes later, she exclaimed, "That IS my sailboat! Who is sailing her?" As they drew closer, she could see a man and a woman aboard. "That's Tony, and Gina. I never told Tony to take her sailing," she told the rail. She remembered how, before she and Tony became an "item," Gina tried to discourage Alex by telling Nora she was engaged to Tony. Lately, Gina had been more friendly, making Alex think she had given up on Tony. On one of Alex's visits to Tony at the airport, Gina had told her that she had a gentleman friend who was taking her to Paris in October.

La Barca's path took her within a hundred feet of the *Golden Hind*, and Tony and Gina waved to her. Suppressing the urge to ignore them, she gave a half-hearted wave and returned to her seat in the cabin.

Once on shore, she walked back to the Clinic, retrieved her car, and drove home. Parked near her garage, she saw Tony's car. So, he came here, helped himself to the boat keys, and took that little Minx sailing. "I've had it," she said loudly as she got out of the car. He's just another flyboy. I am done with him. I should have known better.

Her relationship with Tony had not happened quickly. Both were nursing old hurts, Tony over his ex-wife's disloyalty, and Alex, who during her years of widowhood had had three disastrous relationships with pilots and a man in her Cobury, Maryland theater group. Not even considering that there might be a rational reason, Alex fell back to her distrust of men and said aloud, "Men are all alike, and I am through with Tony and any others."

Walking into her house, she took a large black garbage bag, went up to her bedroom, and put anything of Tony's in it. Tying it up, she took it out and placed it on the trunk of his car. "Good-bye, and good riddance," she said, adding, "I got along before I met you, I'll get along without you now."

Returning to the house, she made a stiff vodka tonic, took some cheese from the refrigerator, put it on a plate, added crackers, and brought them to the porch. She could see La Barca coming up the channel from Lake Michigan to her dock. "Those finks,' she said aloud. She returned to the house and sat on the sofa facing the fireplace. Shortly she could hear footsteps on the steps to the porch. Tony and Gina walked in, and Tony said, "Thanks for letting us use the boat. Gina had never been sailing before."

"So, of course, you left me on the mainland to take her for her first sail." Sarcastically, she added, "Isn't that sweet?" Changing to a very demanding tone, she said, "Tony, put the boat keys on the table and leave my house keys with them. And then get out of here."

"Alex, what is wrong?"

"You know what's wrong. Leaving me after I asked you to wait, and then having the gall to take my boat. Get out, now and forever. Your things are on your car, including your apartment keys."

"Alex, I can explain,"

"I bet you can. Save your breath. I'm not interested. Leave now and take your woman with you."

Realizing that, at this moment, there was no reasoning with Alex and embarrassed that this exchange took place with Gina present, he placed the keys on the table and left.

Once she heard the car drive away, Alex took a gulp of her drink and let her tears fall. Her stomach felt like she had swallowed rocks. After a few minutes, she grabbed a tissue, wiped her face, and berated herself for ever thinking a flyboy could be faithful. Why did I ever let myself fall in love with him? Will I never learn? Better to find out now, she thought. To think her father had trusted him. It shows how little he knew him despite many flights with him as his copilot.

Thinking that she should check La Barca to be sure Tony and that woman had safely secured her, she took her drink and the boat keys and descended to the dock. Stepping aboard, she unlocked the hatch and went below. Whatever those two had done, the scene below decks was neat and as she had left it. Locking the hatch again, she checked all the lines, finding them as they should be. At least they didn't hurt anything. Aloud she said, "Just me. But I don't count."

Sitting on a cockpit bench, she took a long drink as the tears started again. If only Mrs. Bailey had not had that attack, that woman would not have had a chance to go sailing in my place. "Never again will I trust a flyboy or any man," she told the boat. Despite Gina's saying that a gentleman was taking her to Paris this fall, whoever he is, or even if he exists, she was sure Gina had not given up on Tony. "She can have him," she told the boat's cockpit."

An hour later, feeling the chill of the evening, Alex left the boat. Once in her house, she made another drink, sat down, and turned on the TV. A commercial for one of the Rabbit Island restaurants was on. Maybe she'd go out by herself. Then she thought better of it. She might run into Tony and Gina. "I'll fix something here when and if I feel like eating," she told the commercial. Instead, she decided to try to sleep, hoping she could.

Waking up Saturday morning after a restless night, Alex remembered that today Tony was supposed to give her another lesson flying the multi-engine plane. "Sorry, Dad, I won't be getting my multiengine license here on Rabbit Island with that flyboy," she told the bed. She had spent the night tossing and turning, angry at Tony, and sad that their relationship was over. She had hoped that this time her romance was for real.

Her phone rang. "Darn, it's downstairs. Let it ring. If it's Tony, I'm not going to answer." Finally, it stopped ringing, then started again. "Nurts ," she said, dragging herself out of bed. "I'm going to turn that stupid thing off." Retrieving the phone, she saw it was Miss Maggie.

Miss Maggie was her landlord. To persuade Alex to take the job at the Clinic, she told her she would rent her this house with the promise that she could buy it after a year. It was a lovely house, sitting high above Lake Michigan and with everything she needed. An added attraction was the private channel from Lake Michigan with a boat dock.

The house fit well with Alex's desire to have a place of her own. Even if there had been no budget decrease at the Health Clinic in Cobury, which had caused her to be laid off, she might have been tempted to take this job just for her own house. Twenty years in the Air Force with more moves than she wanted to remember and only a little more than two years at Cobury had made her want a permanent place.

Alex knew she could not avoid Miss Maggie, who was well-known for being insistent. If she didn't answer, Miss Maggie would come down and let herself in. Reluctantly, she picked up the phone."

"Have you had breakfast yet?"

"Not even coffee," Alex replied.

"Minnie has just made her famous coffee cake. It's warm, just out of the oven, and the coffee is ready, waiting for you to join us." Minnie was Miss Maggie's housekeeper, and friend.

"I'm not even dressed and I'm not in a good mood."

"All the more reason to come up. I'll give you twenty minutes before I come and get you."

Disconnecting the call, Alex sighed. Fighting Miss Maggie was almost always a losing battle. She's probably already heard about my breakup with Tony and wants to know more. She never misses a thing.

Fifteen minutes later, Alex dragged herself up her driveway to Miss Maggie's. Usually, she would have appreciated the evergreens and sugar maples lining the driveway that were beginning to show red, but today, her mind did not have room for appreciation. Even the east and west views of Lake Michigan, which Miss Maggie's house on the island's south end had, failed to get her usual appreciation. Just before the twenty-minute deadline, she entered Miss Maggie's house.

8 BRUNCH

"Welcome," Miss Maggie greeted Alex. "Have a seat at the table. I've just fixed you a cup of coffee the way you like, with cream and sugar." Despite the time only being nine-thirty, Miss Maggie, somewhere in her seventies, had her silver hair in a French twist and was neatly dressed in gray slacks and a coral blouse with a matching belt. Some women look elegant with silver hair, others just old. Miss Maggie belonged to the former category.

"You look down in the mouth," Miss Maggie told her.

"I guess I am. " After taking a bite of Minnie's coffee cake and a sip of coffee, she finally said, "I suppose you heard that Tony and I are through."

"This morning, when I talked with Julie Goodson, she mentioned that she had been told that Tony and his administrator and pilot, Gina Wistel, had dinner at the Busted Jib last night." Julie was the wife of Steve Goodson, who owned the famous Steve's Island Resort. "She hoped you were ok."

"Oh, I'm ok, physically," Alex said, her coffee cup in her hand.

"But not emotionally?"

Setting down her cup, Alex replied, "I might as well tell you why we broke up if you don't already know."

"I don't know, and I'm sorry if you are."

"Sad, but I'm afraid, not surprised. He's a flyboy. Yesterday, after we took a patient to Crescent City General, I asked him to wait for me, and he said he would. Despite that, he flew away without me. To add insult to injury, he helped himself to my sailboat and took that Gina sailing. I saw them as I was returning on the *Golden Hind*."

"I had heard that Gina's romance had ended. Apparently, her rich boyfriend was married and was using her."

"Too bad, so sad. So, now she has decided to go for Tony instead. My sympathy for her is not measurable." Saying that she took a big bite of the coffee cake, followed by a swallow of coffee.

"Understandable. Are you more upset about breaking up with Tony or about him being with Gina?"

"What's the difference? Anyway, I was fine before we were together, and I will be fine now."

Miss Maggie was also unhappy about the break-up. She had hoped the romance would lead to a marriage and tie them both to Rabbit Island. She knew Alex and Dr. Gould were now working well together, but she always felt a little uneasy about Alex's commitment to Rabbit Island. "I have an idea. How about joining me tomorrow for one of those famous brunches at Steve's Island Resort? I want to see Julie anyway, and it will be good for you."

"I don't want to. I won't be good company."

"Give yourself a good talking to and come with me. You need to do this. Besides, this week Brittany Prince is performing there nightly. Seems she enjoyed the island so much last month when she did the concert for us that she eagerly accepted Julie's invitation to do some shows here."

Knowing Miss Maggie would keep after her until she agreed, Alex reluctantly asked, "What time tomorrow?"

"I was thinking nine-thirty. I'll make a reservation. And

try to wear something you like that will cheer you up."

"I'll try, but don't expect too much from me."

After returning home and trying to forget about Tony, Alex decided to take La Barca for a sail. She made a sandwich, took some water from the refrigerator, and went down the steps to the boat. Before long, she was in Lake Michigan, had raised the sails, and was taking advantage of the west wind. Surprisingly, she found she was enjoying the sail. The wind blew about eight miles an hour, and La Barca easily responded to commands. The soft rhythmic sound of the water against the hull was calming.

A few hours later, she ate the sandwich and opened the water bottle. Finishing her snack, she noticed that the wind had gradually strengthened. Looking to the west, she saw what looked like suspicious clouds. Checking the radar on her phone, she found thunderstorms in the west. It was time to turn back.

The sky became darker as she sailed back. Wanting to be prepared if the storm hit before she was safely at the dock, Alex started the engine, furled the jenny, took down, and covered the mainsail while keeping an eye on the western sky, where she saw lightning. Under power it did not take long before La Barca was chugging up the channel to her dock.

Just as Alex finished making the boat fast at the dock, the skies unleashed a torrent of rain, as what seemed like nonstop lightning lit the sky, and thunder sounded an incessant noise. Not wanting to get any wetter, she rushed through the hatch, descended to the cabin, closed the hatch behind her, and retrieved one of the towels she kept on board.

The boat, even in this enclosed space, pulled at the lines as the movement of the water, together with the wind, caused it to rock. She dried herself and sat on one of the sofa benches to wait out the storm. The stress of hurrying back to her dock to beat the storm erased the relaxation she had earlier achieved. The fury outside seemed to match the fury she felt about Tony's leaving her, sailing with that woman in La Barca, and then having dinner with her at the Busted Jib.

Rat that he is, he knew that news would be all over the island. He was cementing their breakup. Good, she thought. And I'm going to show him I will do fine without him. I'm glad Miss Maggie has invited me to brunch tomorrow at Steve's. I will put on a show of happiness that will fill the gossip mills and make them think I'm happy to have broken up with Tony and that I engineered it. The storm finally moved east, and Alex, still wet from making the boat secure at the dock, locked the hatch and climbed the stairs to her home.

Sunday morning, as Alex walked with Miss Maggie through the lobby into the Steve's Island Resort restaurant, she was working hard to keep her promise to look happy. She had dressed carefully, choosing the aqua dress which was becoming to her, and the pearls that her late husband, David, had given her for their wedding. The maître d' led them to a table with a Lake view.

As the maître d' was seating them, Alex glanced around and saw Tony and Gina in a far corner, as if they were hiding. They should hide, she thought. She didn't lose much time getting him to take her here.

"Would you like coffee?" the waiter inquired.

"Yes," they both said in unison.

"Do you see Tony and Gina over in the corner?" Alex asked.

Glancing there, Miss Maggie answered, "Don't let them get to you. You are here to celebrate, remember. What do you plan to eat?"

The two spent the next few minutes studying the lengthy menu. "Too many choices," Alex said in a bright voice.

"Alexandra Middleton!" a voice said as a tall man approached their table. "What are you doing here?"

Standing up to greet him, Alex said, "Peter Herrison. I might ask you the same thing."

"Let me see you?" Taking both her arms, he moved an arm's length away and said, "You're as beautiful as I remember. Give me a big hug and kiss for old times' sake, and then I'll tell you."

They embraced for a little longer than one would expect with casual acquaintances. He released her and told her, "I'm here with Brittany Prince. Understand she did a fund-raising concert for you last month. Now, who is this lovely lady you are with?"

"Still the old charmer, eh?" Turning to Miss Maggie, Alex said, "Miss Maggie, I want you to meet Pete Herrison. Although, if memory serves me correctly, he now goes by Pete Harris. We went to high school together and were pretty much an item before he became a big star. I'm sure you've seen him in his TV show, Quinn Cass, PI."

Miss Maggie stood up and extended her hand to Pete. "Mr. Harris, I'm charmed to meet you. I didn't realize Alex had such famous friends."

"Can I join you?" he asked.

"Of course. We haven't ordered yet, except for coffee."

Alex glanced over at Gina and saw her looking open-mouthed at them. Pete couldn't have picked a better time to appear, Alex thought as he sat down in the booth beside her and put his arm around her. She smiled at the thought that Gina was probably jealous.

A waiter delivered coffee to all of them and asked for their orders. "This is on me," Pete announced to the waiter. "Ladies, order anything you want."

"That's very kind of you, Mr. Harris, but I will take care of it."

"Miss Maggie, I want to. It isn't every day I get to breakfast with two such elegant ladies." After the waiter took their orders, Pete turned to Alex and asked, "Now it's your turn. What are you doing here with this lovely lady?"

"I live here, as does Miss Maggie."

"How did you end up here? I heard you got married. Where is your husband?"

"Pete, that's a sad story. He's been gone sixteen years now. He was killed in an accident with our two-year-old son."

"I'm so sorry."

"I kept his name, and now I'm Alexandra Lawson. How about you? I can't say I keep up with the fan magazines, but I don't recall reading anywhere that you got married. Did I miss something?"

"You didn't miss anything. I never got over you," he said, looking at her with a flattering smile."

"Yeah, right, with all those Hollywood starlets around."

"They're not all they're cracked up to be. Now tell me why you are here in the middle of Lake Michigan. I know it's an island, but it's much larger than the one you called home near Portland, Maine." Turning to Miss Maggie, he said, "Miss Maggie, Alex and I were more than an item. We were practically inseparable. Our senior year, we were king and queen of homecoming at Portland High." Turning to Alex, he asked, "Why did you leave me?"

"Leave you! That's a laugh. You left first, went to New York to try your luck on Broadway, and never wrote. I went to the University of Michigan and figured you had other things, and other girls, on your mind. Never being home again at the same time, I think we just drifted apart as we got on with our lives."

"I never really got over you, but we did pursue different paths. I should have written, but all my energy was in making it. And you didn't write either."

"I didn't have your address."

"However, I did have some luck on the stage, I thought

you would have heard. It was in the local paper."

"Perhaps when I was in Ann Arbor. Dad never told me."

"Then I was accepted at the Strasburg School of Acting and, as you know, ended up in Hollywood. Never a big star, but I stayed busy. When this TV deal came along, I was in a slump and jumped at the chance. I know it types me, but the money is good, and the work is steady. We're in our third year and have a good audience share, enough so the network is not canceling us. With luck, there will be residuals for reruns after we get canceled."

"I get a chance to watch it now and then. You have good stories, not just car chases, and what I call 'shoot'em up bang bang.' And you are not afraid to tackle some tough subjects."

"I think most of the audience likes that, but we get some hate mail."

"There are always those who want to pretend those issues don't exist and get upset when the light is shined on them."

"That's what our producer thinks, and those folks are watching, which is the bottom line."

Looking at the Lake, Pete Harris commented to Alex and Miss Maggie, "This is a beautiful spot."

"I know, "Alex responded.

As the waiter returned with their coffees, Pete asked, "Alex, tell me, what do you do on this island?"

"I'm a certified nurse practitioner at the Rabbit Island Health Clinic. I have a Doctor of Nursing degree. I can use the title doctor, but outside my professional life, I don't."

The waiter then asked for their orders. Ordering last, Pete ignored Miss Maggie, who had asked to put all the orders on her bill, saying, "I can't let this lovely lady pay. Put these on my tab."

Smiling to herself, Alex wondered if Miss Maggie would rise up and contradict him. Surprisingly, she only said, "That's very generous of you, Mr. Harris."

"Alex, what do you do in your free time? Any men in your life?"

"No to the last question, but I have a sailboat and often take it out on the lake. How about coming for a sail with me?"

Before he could answer, Brittany Prince appeared, saying in a semi-accusing voice, "I see you aren't wasting any time getting to know the island ladies.

9 WEEKEND REQUEST

Despite the sunny and pleasantly warm weather outside this late September day, the atmosphere in the dining room at Steve's Island Resort turned chilly as Brittany Prince stood looking at Pete Harris, who had his arm around Alex. Trying to rescue the situation, Pete said, "Brittany, I want you to meet a lady from my past. Alex Middleton, now Lawson. We grew up together."

Alex reached for Brittany's hand, which was not forthcoming, dropped her hand, and said, "Ms. Prince, I'm delighted to finally meet you. I was too busy when you did the concert for us, and fortunately, you did not need the first aid tent. You're one of my favorite singers. I understand you are performing here at the hotel. Rabbit Island is lucky that you are here."

"Alex, would you like to attend tonight's performance?" Looking at Brittany, Pete asked. "I'm sure Brittany will be glad to have you."

Seeing Pete's arm still around Alex, Brittany did not look thrilled at the suggestion, but politeness kept her from saying anything.

"And," Pete continued, "that lovely lady over there is Miss Maggie. Brittany, why don't you sit next to her?"

"Miss Maggie, I remember you from the concert," Brittany said with forced friendliness as she sat down. "You made sure everything worked smoothly that day. I'm sure it wouldn't have gone as smoothly if you had not been there. It's very nice to see you again. I hope you will accompany Alex tonight?"

"I would be delighted to."

The waiter appeared with their orders and set them on the table. Seeing Brittany, the waiter asked, "Ms. Prince, what would you like?"

"Just a cup of coffee. I have to keep my weight down."

During breakfast, Pete regaled them with tales of his and Alex's escapades during high school. "Remember when you overloaded your boat with our gang? Your dad was pretty upset, wasn't he?"

"Upset is a mild term. Furious is more like it. He said I was not mature enough to appreciate the safety issues of overloading a boat and grounded me for two weeks. As further punishment, he made me study a book on boating safety and then tested me on it."

"I still found a way to see you, didn't I?" Pete said with a mischievous smile.

"You'd have been toast if Dad had ever found out."

"Ah, but he didn't. You managed to keep quite a few things from him, right? If I recall correctly, your older brother, Nelson, once smuggled you to the mainland to see me when your dad was out on one of his trips?"

"Yes, he did," Alex said with a smile. "Luckily, Mom never found out either."

"Brittany, we were quite an item then. Had lots of fun, didn't we?" Pete said. Brittany looked anything but happy at this information.

Seeing Brittany looking annoyed, Alex said, "We did, but that was long ago. Until this morning, I hadn't seen Pete for at least twenty years."

"My loss! You get prettier with each year," Pete said,

smiling appreciatively at Alex.

From the corner of her eye, Alex saw Tony and Gina get up and approach them, appearing to want to be introduced. Alex ignored them, instead turning to Pete and Brittany, saying, "Would you both like to go for a sail with me this afternoon?"

"I can't," Brittany said, adding, "And Pete, I need you to help me rehearse for tonight."

Not being acknowledged, Gina and Tony walked to the lobby's exit as Pete said, "Guess we'll have to take a rain check, but I'll see you tonight a little before eight. I'll fix it with management and get you a seat in the front."

"That is very thoughtful of you, Mr. Harris," Miss Maggie said.

"Please call me Pete like everyone else does."

Returning to her house, Miss Maggie said, "Now, aren't you glad you agreed to come?"

"I mean to admit it, but I loved wiping Gina's face in it. She was dying for an introduction."

"Don't get too cocky, young lady."

"Yeah, she still has the guy."

"Have faith. You know, I think Pete is still soft on you. And I think Brittany sensed it. When he said he never got over you, there was a hint of truth that did not look like acting. Now go home and make yourself pretty for tonight."

"How about I drive tonight?"

"If you'd like. You've been on the island long enough to know the way, even at night."

"I'll stop by for you at seven-thirty."

"I'll be ready."

Entering the hotel that evening, Alex's smile was genuine. It had been a real boost to her self-confidence to see Pete again. Maybe she had never completely gotten over him. Early romances were not that easily discarded. Pete met them in the lobby and escorted them to the promised front table. She hoped the Rabbit Island gossip mill would spread the story that she and Miss Maggie were guests of Pete Harris at one of Brittany Prince's concerts.

During Brittany's performance, she sang many of Alex's favorites, and Alex enthusiastically applauded. For her last song, Brittany walked over to their table and, pointing directly at Alex, sang, with more feeling than necessary, "You Ain't Woman Enough to Take My Man."

Alex was mortified. Pete scowled at Brittany and tried to motion for her to back off, which she eventually did, but not before Alex was the focus of all eyes in the audience. Now, instead of wanting the gossip mill to work in her favor, she hoped most of the audience were tourists who had no idea who she was.

When the song ended, Pete rose instead of waiting for Brittany to come to their table and said, "Let's go."

Alex needed no further invitation. Pete put his arm around her and escorted her and Miss Maggie to their car, apologizing. "I don't know what got into her."

"It was a good performance," Miss Maggie said, trying to lighten the mood. "Isn't that what it's all about? Putting on a show? And Alex was a beautiful foil. Thank you for arranging this. We enjoyed it."

The following Tuesday, Alex saw Ann Hooper at the grocery store. A former Air Force colleague, she was now a nurse practitioner student. After greeting her, Alex asked, "How are you coming with your nurse practitioner studies?"

"Progressing. I'm so glad I ran into you. I wanted to ask you if you would mentor me at the Clinic?"

"I would be pleased to. But I thought Dr. Gould was going to do that."

"Part of the time, yes, but I want to see how you do things as a nurse practitioner, not as a doctor."

"When would this start?"

"January or February of next year."

"I think it can be arranged. I'm so glad you are doing this. We are busy with the influx of new residents who have discovered that the Clinic provides good care. We can use you."

"Thanks, Alex. By the way, I heard about your act the other night at one of Brittany Prince's performances. I understand you played your part perfectly."

Nonplussed, Alex looked at her. Not wanting to share that Brittany's part was not an act but honest, she said, "I love to please."

The rest of the week was very busy at the Clinic. Returning home that Friday, Alex breathed a sigh of relief, set her computer case on a table, poured herself a glass of wine, walked to the porch, and collapsed in exhaustion. Today, everyone and their brother, including her, she was sure, half the Rabbit Island tourists, were positive they needed to be seen at the Clinic before the weekend. Relaxing while enjoying the view of Lake Michigan, she was startled to hear her phone ring. She had left it inside and had to retrieve it. She did not recognize the number but threw caution to the wind and answered, saying, "Hello."

"Alex, this is Pete Harris, or Pete Herrison as you used to know me."

"Pete, to what do I owe the pleasure of this call?"

"Alex, I was hoping you could visit me over the Columbus Day weekend. It's a three-day weekend, and if you can get the time off, I'll send you a ticket. We can reminisce about old times. I miss being able to share some of the old days with someone who was there."

"Pete, that would mean two days in the air for only two there."

"I thought if you could get that Friday off and leave

Thursday evening, we could have three days, not one. I'd love to show you this area."

"It's a long way to go for a weekend."

"But it's doable."

"What about Brittany? Even though we are just old friends, I feel she would not appreciate me coming."

"She's history. We broke up. She said I was overbearing and made too many decisions without consulting anyone. And she was becoming too possessive. I am still upset at how she treated you that night."

"You needn't be. The residents there thought it was all part of the show. Are you sure it wasn't?"

"No, it was Brittany being Brittany. She did not like that we were old sweethearts. Not that she doesn't have a few herself. Anyway, I think she was relieved when I called it off. As I was leaving her place, she said, 'You want to see that nurse on Rabbit Island that you grew up with again, don't you?' She was right."

Alex was puzzled. She didn't know how to feel, elated that Pete wanted to see her again or wondering if she was just a temporary replacement for Brittany. And was going to see him to show Tony that she didn't need him? And maybe make him jealous. Smiling, she thought it would make Gina jealous, thinking she had a famous boyfriend. With these conflicting thoughts, she hedged and said, "I don't think I can get all that time off. I do have a job, you know. One I love."

"You won't know if you don't ask. Please do, and then call me the minute you find out. I'll be waiting for your call. Meanwhile, I have to study my lines. I'm back at work, too, but I have been promised a weekend free on Columbus Day or Indigenous Peoples' Day if you wish. Take care, Alex."

With that, he disconnected as Alex tried to assimilate the situation. Did she even want to fly to California for a weekend? That was all stuff she had done in her younger years, but now, was she prepared for the double time change? Dr. Gould will never let me off, so it won't be a problem.

As she was mulling this over, her phone rang again. This time, it was Miss Maggie. She could not have learned about her last phone call, could she?

"Alex, how about joining Minnie and me for dinner? I have some great news for you."

"I'm pretty tired."

"Nonsense, we will expect you in twenty minutes."

Knowing it would be easier to go than say no, Alex replied, "OK, I'll be there." She wondered what good news Miss Maggie could have for her.

Once Alex was seated in Miss Maggie's living room with a glass of wine in her hand, Miss Maggie smiled and announced, "I know you'll be happy to hear this, but the money we made on the concert together with the Council's contribution will allow us to buy an EHR for the Rabbit Island Clinic."

"Miss Maggie, that is wonderful. But we are going to need help to get it installed and running. Is there any money for that?"

"Did you think I would not have thought of that? Yes, we will have enough money to have an expert help us get started. I'm thinking we should get someone from Downstate to help."

"I just hope they can spare someone."

"And, Alex, there will be someone here Wednesday to see about installing the hardware."

"Wow, that quickly. Does Dr. Gould know?"

"Yes, I told him."

"Then I guess I'd better see about getting our expert from Downstate. I'll do it Monday."

10 THE EHR

Monday morning, as Alex entered the clinic's break room to get a cup of coffee, she was greeted by Dr. Gould. He said Miss Maggie had told him that the financing for the EHR was okayed, and the hardware would be installed this week.

"Miss Maggie told me last night. She sure didn't lose any time getting it started did she? Makes one suspect she had this all arranged a while ago."

"One could get that idea," Dr. Gould said. "I only hope we are ready."

"I plan to contact Downstate today and see if they can spare someone to teach us how to use it."

"Good. By the way, what is your relationship with that TV star Pete Harris?"

"Old friends renewing acquaintance. Why?"

"Gossip has it. It's more serious than that. I heard Brittany was pretty miffed at finding him with his arm around you. And I suspect Tony was none too happy about that either."

With a disgusted look, Alex explained, "Dr. Gould, Tony broke up with me, not vice versa. If he's jealous, good!"

"Ok, ok, I'll not get into your romantic life. But I hope you don't pick up and move to California. I'm enjoying the lessened workload you have made possible, and I don't want to start looking for help."

"It's not going to happen. I like working at the Clinic and with you, and I'm not ready to start anew again!"

"I still wish you were back with Captain Hamilton."

"We have to take things as they are, not how we wish they were. And currently, I have no romantic interests. However, Pete has asked me to visit him for the Columbus Day weekend. We're usually closed that Monday, but could I also have that Friday off?"

"You're not interested in Mr. Harris, correct?"

"In romantic involvement with Pete, no. We live in different worlds, but I would love to see how his world works."

"I see. It's against my better judgement, but if you took call this weekend and worked both Friday and Monday, plus call on a weekend later in October when my wife and I want to visit the Smoky Mountains to see the color, I think it could be arranged. Just promise me you will return and stay here on Rabbit Island?"

"That is my plan. I appreciate this."

"Have a good time. Now, let's get to our patients before Nora gets upset."

Hearing this last exchange, Nora said, "You are at that limit!" Then she added, "Alex, you have Mr. Hopkins in room two for a check-up. His wife is with him. Seems you are the only one they want to see."

Alex met Mr. Hopkins last March during her first visit to Rabbit Island. He was then a post-heart attack patient who was finding it challenging to attend cardiac rehab at Crescent City General. Because of the winter ferry schedule, attending required him to spend a whole day in Crescent City, and he was inclined to not go. Dr. Gould had left Alex with him, and she had talked with him about the need to attend. Not wanting to spend the day in Crescent City but believing Alex that he needed the rehab, he asked why he could not do the cardiac rehab using Zoom. The result was he became involved in starting a Zoom cardiac rehab group on Rabbit Island.

"Thanks, Nora. Have you got his record?"

"Yes. I did the weight and blood pressure and drew a blood sample to send to the lab for cholesterol. Here are the weight and blood pressure results and the cholesterol reading from the last visit."

"Thanks."

Entering the exam room, Alex said, "Good morning, Mr. and Mrs. Hopkins. I must say, you both look wonderful."

"It's all that clean living you taught us," Mr. Hopkins said.

"You taught yourselves and implemented what you needed to do."

"With help from Gwen," Mr. Hopkins replied, smiling at his wife and taking her hand.

"I'm just glad to have him with me," Gwen added.

"Your weight and blood pressure are perfect, and so is your cholesterol. I'm pleased about that."

"So are we," Gwen said.

"How about getting up on the table and letting me listen to your lungs and heart?"

Mr. Hopkins easily positioned himself on the exam table. Finishing the exam, Alex said, "Your lungs are clear, and your heart sounds very healthy. You can plan on at least another ten years if you continue to care for yourself like you are doing."

"He will, I assure you," Gwen said, smiling at him.

"What concerns do you have?" Alex inquired. "It's been only a little more than a year since your heart attack."

"How long am I going to have to take all these pills? I never had to take pills before."

Alex looked at him. "You're not going to like the answer." She paused, "Probably the rest of your life."

"They make me feel like an invalid, and I'm not."

"No, you're not," Alex paused, "it's very likely the pills are keeping you from becoming one. Before your heart attack, you thought you were very healthy, yes?"

"And I was!" he stated emphatically. "But now. . ."

"Mr. Hopkins, before your attack, you had a time bomb inside you. Yet you thought you were healthy. But that time bomb was looking for a time to go off."

Mr. Hopkins opened his eyes wide and acknowledged this with a slight positive shake of his head.

"Now you have a chronic issue that you will need to monitor forever. That can be a tough pill to digest. But others have met this challenge and continued with life. You can, too."

"I know," he paused, "But darn . . ."

"Mr. Hopkins, I've heard that the cardiac rehab you organized on the island will have a permanent home. You have made your condition a positive force for everyone on Rabbit Island."

"It keeps reminding me I'm not healthy."

"Could you have started this program, found a place for it, and continued it if you were not healthy? Accomplishing all this took a lot of effort."

"Honey, you've made, and are making, a great contribution to Rabbit Island with these sessions. When they see me, many spouses, and it's not only men who experience heart attacks, tell me how appreciative they are of your part in getting these sessions started. And they love the support they provide." She paused. "You've told me that it helps to know that there are others like yourself. I'm sure the others in your sessions feel the same way."

"Still, I wish it was like before."

"You mean when you were overeating and being too much of a couch potato," Gwen sternly countered. "I like you better this way. Now we do things together. I've even learned to fish. We walk, sometimes in the Rabbit Island State Park. And I'm not continually having to tell you that you are ruining your health. Are you saying you don't enjoy this?"

"I guess I do, but . . ." Brightening up, he looked at his wife and added, "And I've learned to cook healthy foods that even you like."

Laughing, Gwen said, "And I'm healthier too. Did you know that the post-heart attack support group even has some events for spouses? Gives us a chance to share our stories."

"Glad to hear it. Chronic conditions affect more than the person who is ill. It's easy to forget that." Alex paused and looked at Mr. Hopkins and his wife. "I hope you're proud of your accomplishments, not only in being healthy again but sharing with the community."

"I'm very proud of him," Gwen reported.

"Any questions you would like to ask before you leave?"

"Not today. Will we see you next month? Nora told me you are flying to see that TV star in California. You won't move there, will you? We don't want you to leave us," Gwen said."

Alex took a deep breath and said, "Don't let it worry you. We have just been renewing an old friendship. I grew up with him. Sometimes it's nice to talk with someone who shares the same experiences growing up that you did, especially when your paths took different turns."

"Remember, we need you here," Mr. Hopkins said. "Let Mr. Harris do his TV show from here instead of your moving there."

Alex laughed, "I think you're worrying unnecessarily. Remember, TV stars have a great many women to pick from."

"If he has any brains, he'll pick you."

"Thank you for the compliment, but as I said, do not worry about me leaving. I've just started here, and I don't want to leave. Plus, I'm delighted that we will finally get electronic health records, or EHRs, as they are called. Then, it will be easier for us to transfer patients, and you can check on your health information, too."

"Dr. Gould is okay with them?" Gwen asked.

"To be truthful, he is probably not looking forward to it. Change is always hard. But he can see how they can ease the transition when we transfer patients to either Crescent City General or Downstate. No more waking up at three in the morning, remembering you forgot to pass on some important information about a patient." Alex smiled. Leaving the Hopkins, she added, "See you in three months."

After finishing charting on the Hopkins, Alex called the IT department at Downstate Medical Center and was connected to Eleanor Stephens. When Alex explained her need, Eleanor replied, "We would be happy to send someone to help you. By the way, how far along are you?"

"The hardware installation will be done this week. But we want our system to integrate seamlessly with yours, like Crescent City General's."

"Good idea. I would love to be the one to come, but I need to get permission. Fortunately, we are not implementing anything new now, and I think I can be temporarily spared until the next go-live, which won't be for a month and a half. I'll get back to you shortly. I know we will send someone. It will be easier than cleaning up a mess after the fact, like we had to do at Crescent City General."

"That's what we want to avoid. When do you think you might be able to come?"

"I need to clear this with the department. I don't know who can come, but I'm positive we will send someone."

"We can house whoever comes with the island matriarch, Miss Maggie. She has a lovely house and loves company."

"Ah, yes, I've heard of your Miss Maggie." Eleanor laughed, "A regular bulldozer when she gets an idea."

"You are right on," Alex added. "I see her reputation is more than island-wide. But she is very likable. I'll look forward to your call."

At noon that same day, Eleanor called back. "Dr. Lawson, the department is happy to help you. And I have been elected. Is next week too soon?"

"Of course not. The sooner you are here to help us get the software working, the better we will be. I will assume this will include helping us all learn to work with the system."

"I'll teach you and count on you to teach the others."

"I suggest teaching our medical assistant, Nora, and letting her teach the rest of us."

"Your call. Anyway, I'll see you next Monday. I'll drive up Sunday."

"I'll make a reservation for you and your car on the seven PM ferry. When you arrive, I'll meet you and take you to Miss Maggie's."

That evening, Alex called Pete, "I can have four days over the Columbus Day weekend and can leave early enough Thursday to make the one o'clock Blue Water Flight to Chicago, where I can catch a flight to LA."

"Alex, that's great. On Saturday, we can hang out. Sunday, I want to take you to Catalina Island and show you another kind of island."

"Sounds like fun."

Alex met Eleanor Stephens Sunday evening as she stepped off the *MV Island Queen*. Alex showed her how to get to Miss Maggie's and helped her get settled. Monday morning, she introduced her to Nora and Dr. Gould.

"I'm so glad you could come," Dr. Gould said, surprising Alex, who had expected a little passive aggression. Previously, the doctor only used a computer to email and order tests. However, if he could, he had Nora do that. "I think you will find us ready to learn. I don't want to be left in the past. And we want our patients to have the best care even when we must transfer them."

"I'll try to meet your expectations," Eleanor said, shaking his hand.

After orienting Eleanor to the office, Alex showed her the new system that had just been set up. "I'll get this gear working and then spend a few days setting it up for users. I'll need the password for the office," Eleanor told her.

"Anticipated," Alex said, handing it to her. "After we close tonight, at about five, I'll take you to the local watering hole, the Busted Jib, for dinner. I've already arranged this with Miss Maggie."

Seeing her leave Eleanor, Nora said. "I heard you'll be away over the Columbus Day weekend and are spending it with that TV star Pete Harris. How does it feel to be courted by a celebrity?"

"Nora, I've known Pete almost all my life. To me, he's still Pete Herrison from Portland, Maine."

"Right," she said and rolled her eyes. "By the way, you had a call from a Major Baxter. He said he was a former patient of yours in Iraq. I told him you were busy, and he said he would call you later."

By the time Alex introduced Eleanor to the Busted Jib, he had not called back, and she had forgotten about the call.

***

Neither Alex nor Nora knew that Major Baxter, whose real name was Federico, had no intention of calling again. After talking with Nora, he discontinued the call, turned to Eduardo, and said, "We've found the current location for that nurse. She's a nurse practitioner at the Rabbit Island Clinic."

"Where in the name of creation is Rabbit Island?"

"Let's ask Google. But I think it's somewhere in Lake Michigan."

"How will we get there?"

"The same way others do. There must be ways to get there if there's a clinic there. Now let's search Google for Rabbit Island."

11 PETE HARRIS

As planned, Alex took Eleanor to the Busted Jib for dinner. "I know you've only had a day's experience here, but have you any idea how long it will take Nora to master the system and teach Dr. Gould and me?"

"Nora is doing very well. She has a lot of computer experience, and from what she said, I think she was more than ready for this. She is catching on quickly and, in some cases, has anticipated what to do."

"Any interactions with Dr. Gould?"

"He has peeked in at us a few times, but I think he is a little intimidated."

"Fortunately, he does not want to be considered behind the times, so I believe he will learn. Even now, I think he can see how much easier it will be for us when we transfer patients. All we will need is a transfer note, and the receiving agency can access the patient's record if they need more information."

"Do your patients know this is happening?"

"We put an article in the Rabbit Island Updates. In the article, we explained the privacy safeguards. And only one person asked about this. We assured him that his information would still be secure, just available when needed, but only with his permission. This individual, I think, just wanted to hear it from the horse's mouth."

"It's interesting. HIPAA, or the Health Insurance

Portability and Accountability Act, was created to mandate the portability of healthcare information so that every agency doesn't repeat expensive tests. Privacy was added after public comments, but it sometimes appears that healthcare agencies have seized on the privacy to do what they wanted, keep information private, and pay only lip service to portability."

"My thoughts exactly. However, I'm afraid we're still a long way from a national Electronic Health Record (EHR) for everyone accessible with a person's permission by any healthcare agency. In the military, we had that, and it was wonderful. Wherever you were on a military base, a caregiver had access to your complete health history. It saved lives."

"I doubt we will see that in our lifetimes. Healthcare agencies are still too proprietary. Although good in many aspects, competition shows its ugly side in information sharing."

"I agree. To get back to our local situation, how long do you think you can stay with us?"

"At the rate Nora is going, I think I can safely turn it over to her by the middle of next week. When do you plan to learn it?"

"When I get back from my Columbus Day weekend in California. I'm more fortunate than Dr. Gould. I have had plenty of experience with EHRs, first in the Air Force and then at the Cobury Clinic in Maryland. How is it going staying with Miss Maggie?"

"It's great. She and her housekeeper, Minnie, are excellent hostesses. They have gone out of their way this week to make me feel comfortable. And, as you might expect, Miss Maggie wants a day-by-day account of where Nora is in learning the system."

"It wouldn't be our Miss Maggie if she didn't."

"She seems happy with my reports." Eleanor said.

"Good. Given that her push made this all possible, I

want her to be glad she did it."

Nora proved to be a good learner, and by the day that Alex was leaving, Eleanor felt comfortable that she would do well with the EHR and would be an excellent teacher for Dr. Gould and Alex.

The following Thursday morning, when Alex saw Eleanor, she told her, "I hear you are leaving at noon today. I should be finished by the end of the day."

"Eleanor, I have enjoyed knowing you and watching how patient you have been with Nora."

"If all the people I have to teach were as good as Nora, my life would be a breeze. I've had a very easy time here. And I love your island."

"Come back again as a visitor. I would be happy to have you as my guest, and I suspect Miss Maggie would be too."

"I'll keep that in mind. Alex, it has been nice knowing you. I'll think about a visit next May."

"Great! Meanwhile, thanks for being here. When you return to Downstate, I hope you will not be inundated with what you could not do while you were here."

Alex's afternoon flights had gone like clockwork, and she was in California before seven Pacific time. However, Pete had landed a scene in an upcoming movie and could not get away to meet Alex. Instead, he had a limousine meet her when she landed at the Ontario, California, airport. When the limousine dropped her at Pete's house, or estate, as Alex came to think of it, she was amazed at its size.

As soon as the limo driver had escorted her and her luggage to his door, Pete opened it, saying, "Hi, Beautiful. How was the trip?" Before she could answer, he embraced and kissed her on the cheek."

"It was fine, and so was the limo ride here."

He thanked the limo driver and took Alex's luggage from him. "I was sorry I couldn't meet you, but when I get a chance to play a different role, I have to take it. My series will not run forever, and it's a step away from being typecast.

"It was not a problem."

Entering the house, Alex took a deep breath. "Pete, I can see you have a gorgeous estate."

"I like to think of it as a home. I know it's big, but I have tried to make it homey. I only live in a part of it, and I'm glad to share it with you this weekend. Let me take you to your room. You can freshen up, then come back downstairs. My cook/housekeeper, Alice Seaman, has fixed us a little snack."

"I grabbed a sandwich at O'Hare but am still hungry."

After settling in her room, Alex was pleased she had her own room. It all reinforced in her mind that they were just friends, which, to be truthful, was a relief. Pete had helped at a difficult time by paying attention to her, much to the consternation of Gina. She could only hope Tony was jealous, but why would he be? He was the one who caused their breakup.

The snack that evening was welcome. Much to her surprise, Alex was tired after eating despite Pacific time being three hours earlier. "Pete, I'm exhausted. Will you be okay if I retire now?"

"No problem. I'm a little tired, too. Although movie-making sounds glamorous, it's hard work as well as having an early start. Do you think you can manage not to eat dinner until nine o'clock tomorrow?"

"I think so. See you in the morning."

Pete stood up and walked her to her room, pausing before she entered to hug her. "I'm so glad you could come. We'll have a good time this weekend. I have to work tomorrow, but not until 1:30. How about coming with me? Have you ever been on a movie set?"

"Can't say that I have. It should be interesting."

Alex enjoyed her day on the set. Although Pete

introduced her to some people that she probably should have known, not being an entertainment aficionado, she had to work hard to remember their names. The rest of her time with Pete was a welcome rest for Alex, different from her usual activities. They revived their high school swimming rivalry in Pete's pool, enjoyed an outdoor dinner, and visited Catalina Island. All too soon, it was over.

As they said goodbye, Alex asked, "Pete, could you visit me in a few weeks? The last weekend in October should still be warm, and I would love to entertain you and show you Rabbit Island."

"I'll see if I can free up the time. I'll call you tomorrow."

Returning to work Tuesday morning, Nora and Dr. Gould wanted a report on her weekend. She told them about their trip to Catalina Island, saying that the island had nothing on Rabbit Island except maybe longer tropical weather. But I would rather live here," she said emphatically.

"Did you go to any parties?"

"No. We had a private weekend. I even visited a movie set where he was shooting a scene in an episode in his series."

"What was it about?"

"I was sworn to secrecy. You'll have to wait to see it."

"No sneak preview, eh?" Dr. Gould added.

Laughing, Alex replied, "Correct!"

They were interrupted by Miss Maggie calling Alex and telling her she was expected that evening for dinner. After accepting, Alex said laughingly, "She too wants a play-by-play."

"Alex, I'll have to get you up to speed on the EHR," Nora told her.

"Much to my surprise, I find the EHR very helpful," Dr. Gould said.

"Nora, do we have time in my patient schedule to do that today," Alex asked.

"I think maybe about two thirty." Hearing the outside door of the Clinic open, Nora left them and shortly told Dr. Gould his patient had arrived, and she had put him in room two. Alex refilled her coffee cup and took it to her office, planning to read an article in the latest Nurse Practitioner Journal. Just as she had read the abstract and was starting the article, Nora buzzed her and told her to see her next patient in room three.

The rest of the day passed quickly as one patient after another was seen. Neither Alex nor the doctor had taken time for lunch, and by the time she left the Clinic, Alex was looking forward to dinner at Miss Maggie's. She was still jet-lagged and had not noticed the time but knew she was hungry.

"Well, how's our traveling nurse practitioner?" Miss Maggie greeted her.

"Still trying to get adjusted to the peacefulness of Rabbit Island. But hungry."

"Are you going to stay here or move to California?" Miss Maggie asked, half in jest and half seriously.

"Stay here! Miss Maggie. Don't worry, Pete and I are just old friends and not romantically involved."

"You went a long way to see a friend."

"Yes, and you would too."

"Now tell me the details. What was Pete's house like?"

Between bites of dinner, Alex described the house, her visit to the movie set, and their visit to Catalina Island. Finally, she said, "I'm tired, and I think I've told you everything. Tomorrow is a workday!" She did not tell Miss Maggie about Pete's possible visit last weekend in October. She would find out soon enough.

That evening, as she entered her home, her phone rang. Answering, she heard Pete say,

"I can visit you the last weekend in October."

"Pete, I'm so glad. I love showing off Rabbit Island!

During her lunch break the next day, Alex phoned Julie, the wife of the owner of Steves Island Resort, and arranged housing for Pete while he was on the island. Having dealt with many celebrities, Julie understood the need for privacy and told her, "That weekend, we have an excellent suite available, and as you know, our staff will keep this quiet. Would you like us to meet him at the airport?"

"That would be nice. That will keep the gossip at bay for a while. Thanks, Julie, for thinking of everything."

That evening, Alex called Pete to tell him about the arrangements. "I will meet you in your room after you arrive, and we can enjoy a drink and a little dinner. So don't eat much on the plane."

The following two weeks passed quickly, with Alex smiling to herself about the secret she was keeping from Miss Maggie and everyone else. It was not often that one could keep anything secret on Rabbit Island.

After Julie had Pete settled in his suite at the Rabbit Island Resort, she called Alex to tell her. She and Pete were soon catching up on the last few weeks and enjoying a room service dinner. As Alex left, she said, "I'll call you Saturday morning—maybe around nine. Is that OK?"

"Sure. I'll look forward to it. Alex, it's wonderful to see you again."

She kissed him on the cheek and said, "And for me to see you again! Good night."

Saturday morning, Pete called her at eight-thirty. "Couldn't wait until nine. Where shall we have breakfast?"

"How about I pick you up and bring you to my place, and we have breakfast here? If it's okay with you, we can go for a sail after breakfast."

"I'd like that. I haven't been sailing in years."

The next morning, walking into Alex's great room and seeing her view, Pete said, "I can see why you moved here."

"I'm lucky, I know. How would you like your eggs?"

"Scrambled and with bacon."

Alex put the cinnamon rolls she had purchased in the oven to warm while she fixed eggs and bacon. After they finished breakfast, Alex prepared a few sandwiches and placed them and a few beverages in a cooler she used on the boat. "Are you ready for a sail?"

"Sounds wonderful. If I am any judge of weather, it looks like it will be a perfect day for sailing."

"Your judgment is excellent. There is about a ten-mile-an-hour wind from the south, which the weatherman predicts will move west and strengthen a little. Follow me to the dock." Alex picked up the cooler and started for the door.

"Here, let me take that," Pete said, taking the cooler from her. "What's the name of your boat?

"La Barca de la Senora."

"The Boat of the Lady, how appropriate," he laughed. As they descended to the dock, Pete remarked, "It looks like a great day for sailing."

Once on the Lake, they motored a short way, then raised and set the sails. "We'll go north with this wind. Then we can reach back when the wind hauls to the west."

It was pleasant having a sailing companion. Pete wasn't as good a crew as Tony, but he was a fast learner and quickly learned how to help. During the sail, Alex learned how he landed his current role as Quinn Cass, PI. "I enjoy it, but shooting an episode a week is work! I only have a minor role this week, and we shot that early Friday so I could have the weekend off. Of course, on the flight back, I will study my lines for next week, but I have a photographic memory, so that is not hard."

"I remember how you aced the tests in high school but seemed to rarely study."

"I always wondered if it was so easy to memorize stuff

that maybe I was not learning. I'm logical, so I easily passed multiple-guess tests, but essay tests were my nemesis. Putting the information I memorized into a meaningful answer was hard for me. You excelled at that."

"That is hard for many people."

They were quiet for a while, enjoying the sounds of the water on the boat and the wind on their face. When the sun was directly overhead, Pete asked, "Is it time to eat?"

"I think so. Do you want to sail her while I get the sandwiches?"

"How about I get the sandwiches, and you sail? I've never sailed with a wheel."

"After we eat, you'll have to experiment with it."

"You'll be here in case I make a mistake?"

"You're not going to make a mistake. We'll head back home before I turn it over to you."

After finishing the sandwiches, Pete put the things back in the cooler and went below with them. As he emerged from the cabin, Alex told him, "Pete, I would have done that."

"Hey, no preconceived gender roles here! You were sailing, and it was more convenient for me to do it."

"Anyway, thank you. It's your turn at the helm as soon as we come about."

Not surprising Alex, Pete handled the boat like an expert once the sails had been set for home.

As they secured La Barca at Alex's dock, Pete said, "I want to take you to dinner tonight. I've heard about a lovely restaurant called Reverie in the Woods. "

"I would enjoy that. The leaves should be beautiful."

"If my memory of northern latitudes is correct, won't the leaves be all gone?"

"Rabbit Island does not have the typical northern latitude weather because we are over an unexplained hot spot. Gives us a longer season. And I would enjoy having dinner there with you."

12 LIGHTHOUSE VISIT

While Alex and Pete ascended the steps from Alex's dock to her house, Eduardo and Federico drove their rental car off the *Island Queen.* "Interesting little place," Eduardo said. Where do you suppose she lives?"

As they left the ferry dock area, Federico commented, "The Rabbit Island Health Clinic may be the place to start looking. However, the Clinic may not be open today. Let's go to that Airbnb cabin that we found. It's supposed to be in an isolated spot."

Eduardo, always concerned about his next meal, agreed but added, "As soon as we're settled, can we go into what passes for a town and find a place to eat? Maybe she'll be there."

Federico, always the practical one, replied, "We don't even know what she looks like."

"We'll figure something out. I can't wait to make her give us that thumb drive." He laughed maliciously.

***

Unaware of the new island visitors and wanting to look her best for her date that evening, Alex dressed carefully. Even if he was an old friend, dating a TV star could mean she would be in the public eye. With that in mind, she chose the purple dress that brought out her brown eyes and hair. As she dressed, she asked herself if she was romantically interested in Pete, acting on the rebound from Tony, or just thrilled to be with a celebrity. Or did she want to show Tony that she was perfectly capable of living life without him? And that she could do better than him?

She wondered about Pete's motivation. Was he still carrying the torch for Brittany? She reasoned that Pete's tendency to make decisions for others without consulting the person would not sit well with an independent woman like Brittany. Putting all these thoughts aside, Alex decided just to enjoy the evening and not think about the future.

As she and Pete walked down the walk to Reverie in the Woods, Pete said, "The leaves are beautiful. Is it always this pretty here at this restaurant?"

"I haven't been on Rabbit Island a full year, but so far, I've found that all the seasons have something to make them special. I arrived in April when the mountain laurel was out, followed by the fragrance of the many lilacs on the island. In summer, everything is green. Now it's fall, and you can see how pretty it is. The bright red color you see belongs to the sugar maples. I suspect that when the leaves are gone in the winter, you can see deer and other wildlife here. But the food is the highlight of this place."

"You sound like an ad for the restaurant."

"Perhaps. But it is a treat to be here, although it is a little expensive."

"I had already figured that out," Pete said, smiling. "Nothing's too good for you."

As they entered the restaurant, the maître d said, "Welcome, Mr. Harris and Dr. Lawson. I have your table ready. Follow me, please." He led them to a somewhat secluded table and handed each a menu. They were no sooner seated than the sommelier brought them a bottle of Pinot Noir. He showed it to Pete and offered him a taste. He took a sip and said, "An excellent wine," as the sommelier poured Alex a glass and filled Pete's.

Sipping the wine, Alex said, "It's a Rabbit Island Pinot Noir."

"Your taste has become very sophisticated to recognize not only the type but the origin," Pete said, smiling.

"I'll confess. I saw the bottle and recognized the label. Rabbit Island has some good wines. It's a surprise to all our visitors."

After taking a sip of wine, Pete said, "How do you like living on Rabbit Island? You must be positive in front of the other residents, but you can tell me the truth."

"Pete, it's a good place to be. And I love the house I live in. If things work out, I may buy it next spring. At first, things were a little iffy with the doctor. He had wanted another physician and thought a nurse practitioner would not meet the island's needs, but he has come around, and we now have an excellent working relationship."

"But you're a doctor."

"A Doctor of Nursing, not of medicine. There is a difference." Turning to face Pete, Alex said, "I suspect you preordered the wine. Did you also do the same for the meal?"

"You're on to me."

"I do seem to recall you tend to make decisions for others."

"Are these wrong?"

"Not tonight. I'll admit it saves time, but sometimes people like to be consulted."

"I was sure you'd love the meal. It was recommended by the chef, who I understand knows you."

"Pete, on this island, everyone knows everyone else and their business. By tomorrow, we will be the talk of the town."

"At least it will be positive news, yes? Or are you hiding a gentleman friend who could get upset?"

"Not now." Alex looked away with what looked to Pete like sadness.

"But in the past, yes?"

"Yes, but that's history."

"Want to talk about it?"

"No. Let's say you came at a perfect time."

"My good fortune then?"

"Perhaps."

Just then, their meal arrived. It was the beef dish, one of the restaurant's specialties. "My favorite," Alex said.

"So, my decision was good."

"This time, yes." Alex smiled at Pete as she took her first bite. "I hope you like it as much as I do."

"I'm sure I will. You have great taste."

Enjoying their meal at Reverie in the Woods, Alex and Pete again reminisced about their childhood, especially high school, where they were inseparable. Everyone expected them to get married after graduation, but they both had other goals. "I wish we hadn't drifted so far apart," Pete mused, eyeing Alex.

"I guess we both had different aims. Mine was to eventually become an airline pilot like my dad. Yours was the stage."

"But instead, you went into nursing."

"Dad knew that the airline industry had entered a new era, and pilots could be laid off or strike. He said I needed backup in case either of those happened. And then I met David in his last year of dental school, and well, the rest is history."

"But you never married again."

"There were a few possibilities, mainly pilots. One was killed in an accident, and the other was engaged to three women. In Cobury, there was another, but I soon found out he was married. After that, I was done with fly boys and all men. I've made a pretty good life, probably better than many married women."

"I hope I don't fall into the "all men" category."

"The jury's still out on that one," Alex said, laughing. After Pete settled the bill, she had the valet retrieve her car. While driving to his hotel, he asked, "Alex, will you join me tomorrow morning for brunch at my hotel?"

"That would be a pleasure."

"I'll see you tomorrow at nine in the lobby?"

"I'll be there. Have a good night."

Returning to her house, Alex thought about her relationship with Pete. Was she leading him on, or were the old feelings dormant? How did he feel? She laughed to herself. Perhaps they were just two lost people looking for something they could not describe but hoped to find in each other.

The next morning, as Alex and Pete entered the dining room for brunch at Steve's Hotel, Alex spotted Tony and Gina. Seeing Tony jolted her. That rat, he rarely took me here, but now he brings her here frequently. In her mind, she thought, I'm sure that Gina's jealous of me being with a TV star. Tony is just a stepping stone for her. Under no circumstances will I introduce them.

Settling into a booth with a view of Lake Michigan, Pete asked, "Did you have a good night?"

"Yes, what about you?"

"I think I spent it dreaming about you and how lovely you looked last night."

"Flattery will get you nowhere, but keep it up. I love it, even from an actor."

"Alex, I'm serious."

"Thank-you. Now, what shall we order?"

"Guess what! I'll let you decide for both of us."

"In that case, how about the Mexican Omelet?"

"With a side of juice and coffee?"

"Right on." Turning to the waiter who had just

approached, Alex ordered for them both.

Seeing the coffee pot in the waiter's hand, Pete said, "We'd both love a cup of coffee."

"I remember you both," the waiter, whose name tag read Norris Green, said. "Mr. Harris, yours is black, and Dr. Lawson, you like cream and sugar in the morning."

"Excellent, Mr. Green. I see why you are so popular," Pete told him.

Taking a sip of coffee, Pete said, "My flight does not leave until five this afternoon. What shall we do before then? Of course, I'm assuming you will be with me. Sorry if this decision interrupts your plans."

"Won't that get you back to California pretty late?"

"You forget, I gain three hours."

"I think I can manage an afternoon with you," Alex laughingly said. "After all, I did invite you!"

"Any suggestions for what to do?"

"How about going to the lighthouse and climbing to the top?"

"How many steps?"

"Only eighty-eight. No more than Pete Quinn, PI, can manage."

"I see you read the press releases and know that I do my own stunts, often to the consternation of the producers."

"Why does that not surprise me? You always were a daredevil. Perhaps one of the things that attracted me to you."

Pete laughed, saying, "Ok, you've got me."

As the waiter set their steaming omelets in front of them, Alex said, "I hope you like it as much as I did last night's meal that you ordered."

Taking a bite, Pete smiled and said, "You made a good decision."

"Glad you like it."

While finishing their brunch, Pete turned to Alex and

said, "Now we have to walk this meal off. How far to the lighthouse that you mentioned?"

"From here, probably six or seven miles. I thought we could drive to the St. Haire ferry dock, then walk a mile to the lighthouse and museum."

"Sounds intriguing. Is the lighthouse still functioning?"

"It's operational, but I doubt if, with today's GPS, it is used much for navigation."

When they parked the car in St. Haire near the ferry dock, the *Golden Hind* was at the dock, and passengers were boarding for the 12:30 departure to Crescent City.

"How long does the trip to Crescent City take?" Pete asked.

"In ideal conditions like today, an hour and a quarter. The trip on the *MV Queen* takes three and a quarter hours."

"Do you need a reservation for a car?"

"It's not required, but it is a good idea, especially this time of year."

"Do you take your car when you go to Crescent City?"

"When I go, I usually walk, use public transportation, or rent a car."

Approaching the lighthouse, Pete commented, "I see the light goes off now and then. If my youthful memory serves me correctly, that makes it an occulting light, yes?"

"Your memory is pretty good. This one is off two seconds, then on for five."

"You taught me well when we boated together as teenagers. Every lighthouse has a different pattern, so a seaman knows where they are, right?"

"Yes. You remember well. Let's get our tickets to climb to the top?"

Pete approached the ticket counter and purchased two tickets for the climb.

"Mr. Harris," the ticket seller said. "I had heard you

were in town. I'm glad you brought Alex here; I don't think we've seen her here before. Locals never come here unless they're entertaining guests." She handed Pete the tickets and said, "The last fifty feet, or forty steps of the spiral staircase, is narrow, so you will need to watch for visitors descending. Enjoy!"

Starting up the broad regular stairs for the first part of the climb, they saw a group of visitors leaving. "Was it worth the climb?" Pete asked one of the boys in the group.

"Yes, but I don't know about my parents."

"But they made it?" Alex asked.

"Yes, but they were out of breath a lot."

At the foot of the spiral staircase, several visitors were exiting. "Are there many still up there?" Alex inquired.

"No, we're the last ones."

Slowly making their way up the spiral staircase, they stopped at the window halfway up to look at the lake. The *Golden Hind* had just left the harbor and was starting to plane, shooting water behind her as she gathered speed. "She travels fast, doesn't she?" Pete commented.

"She averages about forty miles per hour but can do sixty."

"Who named her?"

"Captain Hooper, who owns and manages the Rabbit Island Marine Transport. He's a student of marine history and named her after the galleon that Sir Francis Drake used in his 1577 – 1580 circumnavigation of the world."

Reaching the last step, Alex said, "Today is a beautiful day. We should have a good view of the island." They were both silent as they moved to where they could see St. Haire and the island beyond. "Can you make out my house?"

"I see the top of the mast of your sailboat. So, it must be just behind those trees."

"We could probably see it in the winter, but now the

leaves interrupt our view."

Walking clockwise around the top, Pete exclaimed, "I see the hotel. It looks like a big hole just this side of it."

"That's the harbor between the two peninsulas. The hotel is on the end of the west peninsula, or left 'ear' of the rabbit. The golf course is on the right 'ear.' In the harbor between the peninsulas are docks for visiting mariners and a few rental boats."

"I'll have to look from the hotel side when I return."

"I'm surprised you haven't been down to the docks."

"Me too. Usually, I explore more. Next time. Can you rent a boat there?"

"Steve, the owner, has a few, but he's fussy about who he rents to. Which is why you won't see it advertised."

"Let's sit on one of these benches for a few minutes before we go down. I want to relax and enjoy the view."

"Good idea," Alex said as she joined Pete on a bench.

"Look at all the boats. Are they all local?"

"Some are, but most are probably from the Michigan shore which is only thirty-five miles away. There are some possibly from Wisconsin, but that is seventy-five miles to the west."

"So Great Lakes boaters also like to visit other harbors, like you and your family did in the Atlantic."

"One year, when Dad had a vacation, we sailed up to Labrador. Someday, I hope to cruise my boat through the Mackinaw Straits and to the area referred to as the North Channel. It's an inland waterway on the northeast Canadian side of Lake Huron. It's shallower than the Lake and much warmer than the lake itself."

"Where would you dock?"

"There are many places where one can dock or drop an anchor. Many of the islands are rocks, and even sailboats that draw six feet of water can tie up to them like a dock. And they are protected from storms."

"Do you get many storms here on Rabbit Island?"

"Some. The difference in water temperature between most of Lake Michigan and the water around Rabbit Island can create popup storms

Looking at his watch, Pete said, "I suppose we better start down. I don't want to miss my plane. And I want time to explore the museum and the park."

As they were almost at the bottom, a family of four about to start up, waited until they were down. "How is the view?" a young woman asked as their two sons started running up the stairs.

"Boys, stop running; the top is not going anywhere without you," the father yelled after them. "It's not a race."

"I thought it was worth the climb," Pete told the woman.

Turning to Pete, she asked, "Say, aren't you Pete Harris?"

"I've been asked that before. Would love to be him."

As the parents started up the stairs, Alex heard the woman say to her husband, "Honey, I think we just saw Pete Harris, you know, the TV show, "Quinn Cass, PI.""

13 IDENTIFIED

Laughing as they walked away, Pete said, "Pretending not to be Pete Harris when I get asked if I'm him usually works. But in my business, I'm glad to be recognized. I only use this when I don't want to take the time to acknowledge fans. Right now, I'm with you. Our time is limited, and I want to spend it with you."

"I guess I understand," Alex said. Turning to look at him, she asked, "Shall we look at the museum? I hate to tell you that I've never seen it. I hear there is information about two of the shipwrecks that happened near here."

They spent the next hour engrossed in the museum. Pete was particularly fascinated by the story of the Ghost Ship that supposedly helps mariners around Rabbit Island. Text in the museum explained that some radio distress calls sent by boats in trouble resulted in an unexplained rescue before anyone could respond. "Incredible!" Pete exclaimed.

The museum opened to the gift shop, where Pete looked at the offerings. He selected a beautiful blue and gold woman's scarf and purchased it. Alex wondered if he intended it for Brittany.

Outside, they walked in the park surrounding the lighthouse, where several people were enjoying the lake breezes. "Alex, what are you doing here?"

Alex turned to see Ann Hooper with her two sons. "The

same thing you are, enjoying the day."

Unnoticed by Alex, Eduardo and Federico stopped walking as they heard Alex's name, thinking it could be short for Alexandra. Federico whispered to Eduardo, "That may be our woman. Let's stay close for a few minutes."

Ann asked, "Did you climb to the top?"

"We did. How about you Ann?"

"Not this time, I put my foot down. The boys have been up there at least five times this year, and I'm tired of the climb. I worked overtime yesterday at Crescent City General and want to relax today. You've not met our boys yet, have you?"

"I've not had the pleasure."

"Shawn and Craig, this is Dr. Lawson. She will help me become a nurse practitioner like she is."

"Pleased to meet you," Craig said, extending his hand to Alex.

"My pleasure," Alex told him and shook his hand.

Not to be outdone by his older brother, Shawn repeated the performance.

"It's her," Federico whispered as he and Eduardo moved a little further away to avoid attracting attention. There, they nonchalantly studied Alex so they could recognize her later.

"I would like you all to meet Pete Harris," Alex said.

"Ann, I'm delighted to meet you. You have a beautiful island here," Pete said as he shook her hand and greeted the boys, calling each by name.

"We're honored to make your acquaintance," Ann said.

"I'm looking forward to next year when you will be in our office," Alex told Ann. "So glad we ran into you and were able to meet your sons. They are very well-mannered."

"Military background in both Chuck and me, I guess."

"Mom, can we go skip some stones?" Craig asked. Instead of sand, the beach at the lighthouse park had pebbles and rocks, many of which were perfect for skipping.

Saying goodbye as Ann started to follow the boys to the beach, Pete spotted a bench. "Alex, let's sit for a while. There is something I want to show you."

Sitting down, he pulled the scarf from the bag and handed it to her, saying, "I couldn't resist this. It will look beautiful on you."

"Pete, you shouldn't have."

"Should, shouldn't, I wanted to. I've thoroughly enjoyed this weekend with you. Hate to go back today."

Accepting the scarf and draping it around her neck, Alex said, "Thank you very much, Pete. I will enjoy wearing it and think of you when I do."

"I hope so." He then turned to face her directly. "Let me look at you. I want to remember how you look with it on."

That evening, after leaving Pete at the airport, Alex thought again about the weekend. It had boosted her self-confidence the day after Tony had deserted her when Pete had shown up and made such a fuss about her. She knew that his visit with her this weekend was by now common gossip. She did enjoy being with him, but she wondered if not making any future plans was his way of saying, "It was fun, but this is as far as it should go." How could she ever compete against a woman like Brittany or other Hollywood types? To be truthful, she also did not bring up any future visits. Was that her way of ending it? She told herself, "It's best to regard this visit as a wild fling and get on with my single life."

***

Oblivious to Alex's situation, Eduardo and Federico had settled into their cabin. They wanted to keep a low profile, and although they had frequented the Busted Jib and Fisherman's Hole for a few meals, they had purchased groceries and had most of their meals in their cabin. "We were lucky that we were able to identify that nurse," Federico commented.

"Must be a sign that we will be successful," Eduardo said hopefully.

"We know what the woman looks like. Tomorrow, we will go to the Clinic at about 4:30 and watch for her to leave. Then we will follow her and find out where she lives. The next day, when she is working, we will get to her house and see if we can find the thumb drive."

"And deprive me of making her tell us?" Eduardo complained.

"Look, our goal is to get the drive. If we can do it without creating problems, it will be best. You'll have to be content with imagining making her talk."

"Not the same."

"True, but you can remember your past efforts. And in our case, the sooner we get that drive, the better it will be."

"Maybe we'll be unlucky, and we won't find the drive at her house. Then I can have my fun." Eduardo smiled maliciously in anticipation. "I hope we have to make her talk."

Monday morning, Alex, unaware of these plans, entered the Clinic as usual. "Good morning, Miss Celebrity," Nora greeted her.

"Having a weekend with an old acquaintance hardly makes me a celebrity."

"Ah, but you have been cavorting with one."

"If you mean my showing Mr. Harris around the island, I am glad to plead guilty. But that does not make me a celebrity, if anything, a 'hanger-oner'"

"Are you going to leave us and marry him?"

"Nora, nothing could be further from the truth. We have no plans to see each other again."

"But you will, yes?"

"I have no idea. Pete has a job, and so do I. If we see

each other again, it will have to be when we are both free. How are things working with the new EHR?"

"Great. Eleanor helped to put all the current patient records in the system, but they will not be as helpful as what we are doing now because they are organized like our paper records. However, we made a list of each patient's current problem and a notation where more information could be found. The most laborious part was entering the patients' current meds and referencing ones they had taken in the past. It was a lot of work, but Eleanor was great."

"How is Dr. Gould doing?"

"Wonderfully! Once he knew that he could easily access the old records, he learned how easy it is to keep up the problem list and meds and enter notes, he was on board. Do you need a review?"

"You already gave me a little orientation. How about I start using them? If I run into problems, I can ask you. You are a great teacher. And the day after you taught me, I had ample opportunity to use my new skills, and I only had to ask you for help twice."

"Remember, I'm still available if you need it," Nora told her.

Entering the Clinic, Dr. Gould said, "Good morning to our celebrity nurse practitioner. Glad you can take time from your busy schedule to work."

"Dr. Gould, I am glad to work. As I recall, I promised you a long weekend with your wife when you gave me that extra day so I could visit California. Yes?"

"Glad you mentioned it. How about this weekend if it doesn't interfere with your plans? It's your turn to cover anyway, but I thought I would take off Friday and Monday."

"I have no plans, and I would happily accommodate you."

"Good. I'll tell the missus to start packing. I am happy

for you, but I had to do some teasing. My only hope is that you don't leave us." He grinned at Alex.

"Dr. Gould, that is not in the cards. As I told Nora, we don't even have plans to see each other again."

"Well, then we'll have to see that you are happy here. Nora, who have you got lined up for us to see?"

A typical Monday, both Alex and Dr. Gould were busy. Alex, however, was able to grab a fifteen-minute break to enjoy a quick sandwich. She felt good that all her patients were doing well that day and, best of all, they were following the plans they had worked out with her. Maybe everyone wanted to be in the best of health for the coming holidays.

Thursday would be the first of November. She needed to plan to get her boat out of the water for the winter. Her boat cradle had already been delivered to Bert Nelson's marina, and the plan was to take her boat out the weekend before Thanksgiving. She smiled at that. Typically, you want your boat out of the water before Halloween in Michigan.

Unaware of Federico and Eduardo's plans to follow her home to find out where she lived, a little after five, Alex left the Clinic. Having found out about Pete's visit, Miss Maggie demanded she join her for dinner. Knowing there was no way out of this, she drove to Miss Maggie's house, parked, and walked in.

Watching as Alex parked at Miss Maggie's, Federico exclaimed, "Wow, this broad has money. Will you look at this place? Maybe we should kidnap and ransom her."

"I've seen better houses, and not on some dumb island in the middle of a lake," Eduardo grumbled. "Anyway, we'd never see any of the ransom. It would all go to Javier."

"Who knows? Perhaps not if we planned carefully, not letting him know. Meanwhile, we have work to do. Tomorrow, let's, as they say, 'case' this joint and make plans to get inside while she's at work. Is that okay?"

"For now."

"Glad you agree."

"Now we know where she lives. Let's go back to our place and have something to eat. I'm hungry."

"You're always hungry. How can you eat so much and stay so slim."

"Exercise!"

"Hah! Your idea of exercise is using the remote."

Early the next afternoon, answering the door at Miss Maggie's house, Minnie found a gentleman who was surprised to find someone home. "Ma'am, I am Major Hugo Baxter, a former patient of Dr. Lawson's in Iraq. Is she home?"

"I'm sorry she's not here. She's working today. Besides, she does not live here."

"So sorry, I thought she did. Where does she live?"

Not ready to provide that information easily, Minnie asked, "Why do you want to know?"

"She took such good care of me in Iraq when I was injured. I heard she had moved to this island, and I want to thank her personally."

"Perhaps you can meet her at the Clinic."

"Oh, but I want to surprise her at her home," Federico said, giving Minnie his most charming smile. "She is such a special person, yes?" Smiling again in a very personable way, he added, "If you can tell me where she lives, I can buy some flowers and greet her when she gets home."

"I don't know," Minnie equivocated. "You should see her at the Clinic."

"Please," he begged in a persuasive tone. "I've wanted to do this for so long. You are smart to be wary, but I assure you I want nothing but the best for her." Looking very trustworthy, Federico said, "You will help me, won't you?"

Reluctantly, Minnie said, "She lives at the foot of the driveway on the other side of the road just beyond here." She hoped Alex would not mind.

"Thank you, you are very kind. I am very grateful. What time do you think she will get home?"

Sometime between five thirty and six. Depends on how busy the Clinic is."

Giving Minnie a large smile, he again said, "Thank you. Can you suggest where I can buy a dozen red roses for the lady?"

"The florist in St. Haire, about a quarter of a mile beyond the dock. That is the best place."

Giving Minnie a grateful look, Federico went to his car and left.

After he left, Minnie thought the whole thing was strange. She planned to tell Miss Maggie when she came home.

In the car, he told Eduardo, who had been hiding out of sight while he talked with Minnie., "Maybe she's not as rich as we thought. This is not her house, but I found out where she lives. The old lady said she'd be home between five thirty and six. That will give us time to look the house over and decide our best approach.

"I see your stint as Major Baxter worked okay. How about doing it again with Dr. Lawson?"

"That's my plan. Hopefully, that and the roses will get me inside her house. Then later, I can let you in."

"Here's her driveway," Federico said as he turned in and started down. "I hope she doesn't have a security system." Once at the house, he turned the car around and parked it. "Let's look around."

As the two explored the outside, Eduardo said, "From what I can see, this is a nice place, with a good view of the lake. Maybe the ransom idea is a good one. But first, I get my way with her."

"First things first, eh?" Federico quipped.

"Hey, how about that sailboat at the dock down there?" Eduardo said. "Maybe we can use that to take her off the island."

"And leave the car here? No way. We can't leave a trail. Besides, neither of us knows how to use a boat on a big lake, like this one. "

"Let's return around seven thirty, and I'll do the Major Baxter routine again."

"First, some dinner. How can I be good at my trade?" he stopped and grinned evilly, "On an empty stomach."

"Your stomach again, always thinking of food."

14 KIDNAPPED

That evening, before driving down her driveway, Alex stopped at her mailbox at the head of the driveway and retrieved her mail. Entering the kitchen, she put the mail on the kitchen table and sat down to sort it. "Junk," she said aloud, putting most of it in a pile to recycle. "Good! The October Nurse Practitioner Journal. Looks interesting." After recycling the junk, she rummaged in her refrigerator for something to eat. She had had a late lunch and was not too hungry. Finding nothing, she opened the freezer and took out one of the frozen stuffed peppers she had purchased last week at Mike's General Store.

After quickly removing the wrappings and reading the directions, she put the food in the microwave and poured a glass of wine. Taking her wine, she went into the great room and turned on the TV to see if anything interesting was in the news. It was six o'clock, and the local station summarized the earlier news.

Satisfied that nothing untoward had occurred that day, when she heard the microwave stop, she turned off the TV, returned to the kitchen, retrieved her stuffed pepper from the microwave, put it on a plate, and took it with her wine to the great room where she set them on the table. Dinner finished, she cleaned up, retrieved her new journal, and settled down to read. A half-hour later, she was startled to hear her doorbell ring. Half of her did not want to answer, and she deliberated.

Eduardo and Federico had driven partially down Alex's driveway and left their car out of sight. "She's in there, I know. Ring it again," Eduardo said.

Federico did. When there was no answer, he rang it again, this time with short, insistent rings.

Alex went to the door, believing she would have no peace until she answered. Opening the inside door, through the screen door, she saw a strange man holding a bouquet of roses.

Starting to close the door, she heard, "Wait, please. I'm Major Hugo Baxter. I've brought these roses to you to thank you for the excellent care you gave me in Iraq."

When Alex looked perplexed, he added, "You don't remember me, do you?"

"I'm afraid not."

"May I come in?"

"Not now. Give me ten minutes, and I'll meet you at the Busted Jib in downtown St. Haire."

Ignoring her statement, Federico yanked open the screen door while Alex started to close the inner door. Pushing on the partially opened door, Federico, alias Major Baxter, said, "No. I'm coming in now. I've waited too long to see you, and thank you."

Pushing back on the door, Alex replied, "And you can wait another fifteen minutes and meet me at the Busted Jib."

"I don't know where that is, and I want to get these roses in water."

"Please leave."

"Having a little trouble here," a menacing voice belonging to Eduardo, who until now had been out of sight, rang out. "Let the gentleman in," he demanded in a loud voice.

Alex pushed harder against the door, but was no match for the two of them. Once inside, much to her surprise, Major Baxter asked for a vase to put the flowers in water. Not knowing what else to do, Alex retrieved one from a shelf and filled it with fresh water.

He handed her the flowers and said, "This was all I wanted. You arrange them."

Getting her scissors, Alex ran the cold water and cut each stem to a length that fit the vase. When she was done, Major Baxter, she still thought of him as that, took the scissors and placed them out of her reach.

"Now, Dr. Lawson, let's go sit down. We need to talk."

Working hard to conquer her fear and looking for a way to escape, Alex led the two men to her great room.

'Lovely view you have," Federico said. "This house can't have come cheap,"

"I'm just renting," Alex said.

Showing impatience, Eduardo said. "Now tell us where it is!"

"Where what is?"

"You know. We want it, and we intend to have it."

She looked around and tried to gauge whether she could make it to the door without one of them stopping her. Then she said, "If I knew what you wanted, it would be easier for me to tell you if I had it."

"You have it! We know that.' Eduardo said. "You can make this easy or hard on yourself." He paused and added menacingly, "Your choice."

Thinking fast, Alex said. "All right, I'll get it. It's in a container outside the house."

"Tell me where it is."

"It's easier to show you. You'll never find it without me." Opening the door to the porch, she led the men down to her dock, thinking she could jump in and swim away. She hoped they couldn't swim or wouldn't shoot her. At the end of the dock, as she was about to jump in, Eduardo grabbed her.

"Help me," she screamed, hoping the man in the

fishing boat outside her channel could hear her. Before Eduardo could put his hand over her mouth, she managed to get out, "Kidnapping me. Call the police."

"Don't pay any attention to her," Eduardo yelled back to the man. "She's crazy." With that, he and Federico half pushed and half dragged her off the dock and up to the house. Once inside, Eduardo slapped her hard, giving her a bloody nose.

"Eduardo, forget that now. We need to get out of here. That man in the fishing boat may call the police. And we can't trust her. Get the chloroform. We'll drug her and put her in the trunk and take her back to our cabin. Then tomorrow morning, we'll take her off the island on the six-thirty ferry to Crescent City."

Disappointed, Eduardo said, "Can't I work on her here?"

"It's not safe. Get the chloroform. Once she's out, we'll give her some real drugs."

"No! Please, no drugs,' Alex exclaimed loudly. I am way too susceptible to them. I can't be around them without becoming quickly unconscious. That's why I never worked in the operating room."

"Yea! Right," Eduardo said, clamping a cloth with chloroform over her nose and mouth as Alex let herself slump to the floor. Although groggy, she felt a needle being inserted into her vein. Try as she could, she could not fight the drug, and the two men were soon able to carry her to the trunk of their car, place her in it, and close it.

"That will keep her for about four hours. Then we'll have to give her some more. Meanwhile, we must get out of here before that man calls the police. As they drove towards St. Haire, they heard and saw a police car with flashing blue lights and a siren blaring drive past them.

"Drive faster, Federico," Eduardo yelled. "They'll catch

us."

"Calm down, Eduardo. We don't want to call attention to ourselves. We need to drive naturally," Federico said as the police car roared past them. He paused, concentrating on driving, then said, "We've already checked out, settled our bill, and told them we were leaving tomorrow morning. Once we are at the cabin, we can park the car where we can see it while keeping her drugged. Then, before we board the ferry, we'll give her a real big dose to be sure she is out."

"Are you sure they won't find us?"

"Who will find us? The cops are probably after something else. Maybe that old lady in that house fell or thinks she saw a prowler. They passed us by and did not turn around. As far as they're concerned, we were just another car on the road. Relax, Eduardo, you'll get your chance with her once we're safely off this island."

Shortly, the two men drove into the driveway to their cabin. "Now, let's get some sleep. In about three hours, I'll come out and give our friend some more drugs to be sure she sleeps through the night. Then it will be your turn."

At six in the morning, after giving Alex a strong dose, they left their cabin and drove to the ferry dock, where they joined the line to board the ferry. About fifteen minutes later, they drove on the ferry and parked where they had been directed. The deckhand told them to leave their car and go to the passenger deck. "Can't we stay in the car?" Federico asked.

"No, we don't let passengers ride in their cars. If something should happen, we want the passengers where we can easily get them into life rafts."

"Is that going to happen?" Eduardo asked.

"Highly unlikely," the deckhand told him. "But we have to follow the rules.

Reluctantly, the two left their car and proceeded to the passenger deck, where they sat down. As the ferry pulled away from the dock, Federico turned to Eduardo and said, "See, there was no problem? Let's enjoy the trip like any other passenger."

"Let's go to the café for something to eat," Eduardo said.

"You and your eating," Federico replied.

"You said we should act like regular passengers. Eating is perfectly normal. And I'm hungry."

After buying coffee and a Danish in the café, Federico said, "Let's eat them here where there's a great lake view."

As the duo enjoyed their breakfast, Chief Pauls and the K9 handler, Danny, with his dog, were examining the cars on the car deck below. Suddenly, the dog, sniffing a car, stopped and barked. "What do we have here?" the Chief asked. Finding the car locked but hearing the dog keep up an insistent barking, the Chief, using his tools, opened the door. Finding nothing inside, he used the button to pop the trunk. As soon as he did, the dog jumped up, looked in the trunk, and barked even louder as if to say, "Here she is. What are you waiting for?"

The chief and Danny lost no time looking in the trunk. "She's out like a light," the chief said while Danny rewarded the dog. Lifting Alex out of the trunk, the chief reached for her carotid artery to see if she was still alive. "She's drugged. Danny, get that Narcan out of our car."

Administering the drug, but with Alex still unconscious, the chief said, "We've got to get her to the hospital right away. We can't wait until we reach Crescent City. Get Rabbit Island Air on the line and have them send the chopper. "Turning to the deckhand, who by now was looking on, the chief asked, "Where can I take her?"

"Follow me," he said, leading the Chief carrying Alex to a cabin on that deck with a small cot. After placing Alex on the cot, he turned to Danny. "Keep watch on Alex while I talk to the captain."

After reaching the bridge and explaining the situation, the captain told him, "You will have to airlift her. There is no room for a chopper to land here."

"Have you had any experience with airlifting a patient?"

"Yes, when I was in the Coast Guard. But to do this, we need some experienced help on deck." Turning to his first mate, he said, "Canvas the crew and see if we have anyone with this experience. "This is not a simple maneuver like you see in the movies. It's quite dangerous, more so with an inexperienced crew."

"If we don't try, we may lose Dr. Lawson." With that, the chief went back to Alex. "Did you get Rabbit Island Air to send the chopper?" He asked Danny.

"Yes, they are warming up now. Said to call them using your radio on the chopper frequency."

Hoping his radio would work on the ferry, Chief Pauls found his car, which fortunately was outside on the deck, and radioed the helicopter. "Rabbit Island Air, this is Chief Pauls."

"I hear you," came Captain Hamilton's worried voice. "Is she ok?"

"So far, she's alive. I've treated her with Narcan, but we need to get her to Crescent City General ASAP. You'll have to do it deck lift," Chief Pauls said.

"I am ready for that. I had a suspicion it would be necessary. Luckily, I was able to contact a couple of first responders who have had this experience. They are with me. I can drop them both on your deck first so they can help at that end."

"Good. I don't know if any crew aboard have experience with a helicopter lift. The first officer is canvassing the crew right now. How far away are you?"

"About five minutes out. I see you."

The first officer appeared on deck with a crew member who was a retired Coast Guard Commander and had assisted in air lifts when stationed at the Alaska station. "Thank heavens. With him here, the chopper won't have to drop someone," the chief stated.

Five minutes later, the chief's radio blared, "I see you. Do you need us to drop a first responder?"

"No. We have a retired Coast Guard Commander as a crew. He has experience with this. Right now, another crew member is getting all the passengers back inside to keep them out of the way."

"Have you informed the captain about our plan?

"Yes. It's Captain Martin. We're lucky. He's also former Coast Guard and has done this several times while stationed in Alaska. He is ready to do what you need. I have given him your frequency so you can communicate.

Hearing the chopper, Eduardo rushed to the window and looked out. "Federico, come here."

When Federico saw the chopper and deckhands with life jackets and gloves on, he was concerned. "Eduardo, just stay calm. I can handle this. Let's go to the passenger deck and find out what's happening."

While the helicopter dropped a line known as a hi-line, the former Coast Guard Commander clipped it to a railing along with another wire to discharge any static electricity. Federico and Eduardo crowded near the window with everyone told to stay inside. If the crew had not been near the doors, Federico and Eduardo would have stormed the door. Instead, Federico asked a crew member, "What's the problem?"

"Oh, some guy fell and cut his head. Guess it's pretty serious, or they would have waited a few hours until we got to Crescent City."

"Thanks," he told the man. Then, as a basket for the

patient was lowered, he relayed the information to Eduardo. Everything ready, Alex was lifted into the basket and secured for her trip up to the waiting chopper.

"Look!" Eduardo exclaimed. "That's no man. That's a woman. And she is wearing that dark pink blouse she had on. It's her!"

Federico had noticed the same thing and quietly led Eduardo out of the crowd. "Ok, our priority now is to get off the ferry without causing any concern. We will leave the car and disembark with the walk-on passengers. Until we are at the Crescent City Dock, we'll sit on the passenger deck near the stairway to the gangplank."

After checking that Alex was aboard the chopper and secured, Captain Hamilton immediately headed for Crescent City General as one of the first responders put an oxygen mask on Alex. Gina, sitting in the right-hand seat, told him, "Nice work. I've never seen that done before."

"We were lucky this time. Trained personnel were available on Rabbit Island and on the ship. I don't even want to contemplate the odds on that. Someone up there wants Alex saved," one of the responders said.

"Not necessarily lucky, just people doing their jobs," Gina said.

Captain Hamilton looked at her, shook his head, and said nothing.

When they landed, an Emergency Department (ED) team from Crescent City General was at the heliport, and they quickly transferred Alex to one of their gurneys. One replaced the chopper's oxygen mask with one of theirs, and the team started wheeling Alex to the ED while two nurses were starting IVs, one in each arm.

"Time to go back to Rabbit Island and have some coffee at the office," Gina told Tony.

"No, we can get some here in the cafeteria. I'm not

leaving until I know how Alex is."

"Suppose there's another emergency," Gina protested.

"Then there will be another emergency. Bill Yazzie will have to make do with the fixed-wing plane." Calling to one of the Crescent City General pilots he knew, and pointing at the chopper, he asked, "Can we leave her here for a while?"

"Just taxi her over there," the Crescent City General pilot answered, pointing to a spot.

After parking, Captain Hamilton got out of the helicopter and was followed by an annoyed Gina. Following Captain Hamilton, Gina realized an attitude adjustment was necessary. She was concerned that the captain was still in love with Alex. Once seated in the cafeteria and sipping her coffee, she said to him, "I hope this won't interfere with Alex's romance with Pete Harris. Seems like old loves are the best."

Captain Hamilton looked at her but said nothing. Taking his coffee, he left the cafeteria and started for the ED to see if there was any news of Alex. Not wanting to leave, Gina said loudly, "Hey, Tony, come back. They'll let you know when there is news." Realizing he was not going to stop, she reluctantly picked up her coffee and followed.

15 Reverberations

With Gina following, Tony left the cafeteria after they had rescued Alex from the *Queen* and brought her to Crescent City General. He headed for the Emergency Department (ED) to check on Alex. Introducing himself to the ED ward clerk, he asked, "How is Dr. Larson?"

"I'll ask her nurse to talk with you." As the ward clerk was telling them all the information she was permitted to share, Cathy Benton approached Tony.

Looking at the clerk, Cathy told her, "I'll take care of this." She turned to Gina and Tony and said, "I understand your concern. Right now, it's touch and go, but the doctors are optimistic. She is responding well to their treatment. If you give me your phone number, I'll call you with any updates."

"Thanks," a worried Tony replied, as he gave Cathy his cell number while Gina watched, annoyed that he cared about Alex. After exchanging cell numbers, Tony told Cathy, "We need to get back to Rabbit Island. Knowing that you will keep me updated, I can leave." With Gina obediently following, he headed for their chopper.

"Hey, wait up," Chief Pauls yelled after them. "Can you give us a lift back to the island? We will pick up our car when the *Queen* returns, but now we need to get back.

"I think we can make room for the three of you. Addressing Danny, he asked, "Has your dog had any experience in a helicopter?"

"During his training and he did fine."

"Okay, give us a minute or two to put the stretcher away, and then there will be room for all of you."

***

Early that evening, rescuing their car from the *Queen*, Chief Pauls, or Irv, as his friends called him, thought about their role in this incident. During the afternoon, he heard from Tony that Alex would recover but that she needed to be in the hospital for the night. With this information, he breathed easier. Entering the station, he saw Danny. "Danny, you and your dog were indispensable today. This should put to rest any complaints about the cost of having a K9 unit on Rabbit Island."

"Some good came out of this, I guess," Danny replied resignedly, looking up from a desk as he wrote his reports.

"It's easier to do the work than write about it," Chief Pauls laughingly said. Entering his office to write his report, his phone rang. "Chief Pauls, here."

"This is Mike Benton, the Crescent City Chief of Detectives. I'm happy to tell you we were able to apprehend the two men who tried to kidnap Alex. The deckhand who had told them where to park remembered the car and its occupants and was able to point them out as they attempted to leave the *Queen* on foot."

"That's great."

"However, they've lawyered up, and we may have to let them go this evening. They're claiming they were misidentified. One of them is very suave and persuasive."

"Captain Martin told me that the deckhand who remembered them had an excellent memory and was very sure of the identification. If you have to let those creeps go, it's criminal."

"In our minds, yes. But they need to be proven guilty in a court of law."

"Will they be tried?"

"That hinges on what Alex can tell us."

Disgusted, he disconnected the call only to have his phone ring again. "Chief Pauls here."

"Irv, we've been summoned to dinner tonight at Miss Maggie's," he heard his wife, Camille, say.

The chief laughed, "Not surprised. She wants to hear what happened today from those involved, not some newspaper article."

"I'd like to hear too. Just glad you are okay. Tony and his new girl, Gina, will be there. Can you make it by five?"

"I need to finish the report. Speaking of the newspaper, I had better call Arvin Chesney over at Rabbit Island Updates and give him the scoop. I like to keep the paper on our side, so I cooperate whenever I can. That will take a little time, but I'll try to be home before five so we can go together. If not, you'd better go, and I'll meet you there.

"I understand. I hope you can make it home first."

The chief was lucky. He finished his report just as Alvin came into his office. Irv wanted their role explained positively, including how the dog saved the day, but did not want to tell him that the police in Crescent City may have to let the perps go. Instead, he avoided the issue. An experienced reporter, Alvin quickly assimilated the facts Chief Pauls was willing to tell him and said he would publish it in this week's paper. "We only publish weekly, which is too bad. I imagine by next week, there will be rumors galore. I trust you will keep me advised of the facts so we can counter some of them."

"Of course. Glad you can fit it in this week's issue."

During the cocktail hour at Miss Maggie's, Chief Paul's story had to be told to Miss Maggie's satisfaction. If he left something out, Miss Maggie would ask a question and get the information she wanted. Finally, when he had finished, Miss Maggie turned to Tony and asked, "What can you add to that?"

"Nothing that I or the chief have not already told you."

"Chief, you haven't yet told me how Alex is."

"Mike Benton, his wife, who is the vice-president for nursing at Crescent City General, told me that she will be okay, but that they want to keep her for observation at least tonight. Apparently, those two creeps loaded her with narcotics, including fentanyl."

"I'm glad Alex is going to be okay, but what on earth is this all about?" Receiving nothing but shrugs to her question, Miss Maggie turned to Minnie, "Minnie, I think we're ready to eat."

Instead of responding immediately, Minnie confessed to the group, "After you described those men, I realized I showed one of them where Alex lived. I feel terrible. It's all my fault."

"How is it your fault?" Chief Pauls inquired.

"The tall one. He came to the door asking for Dr. Lawson, said he was Major Hugo Baxter, and said Alex had taken care of him in Iraq and he wanted to thank her personally."

"Minnie, you're not to blame. Sooner or later, they would have discovered where she lived. It was pure luck that Jason Hopkins was on the lake when Alex needed help. Most other times, he would not have been. He called us and said something was up with Alex. When we got to her house, and no one was there, and no one knew where she was, we suspected something," Chief Pauls told her. "Your timing saved Alex."

"Believe him, Minnie." Miss Maggie reiterated.

After dinner, as the guests were about to depart, Chief Pauls' phone rang. "Irv, I hate to tell you this, but we had to let those two go on a bond. The judge set it at $250,000 each, but that was no problem for their lawyers. They should have waited until we talked to Alex, but cartel lawyers are good and have some powerful people on their side. I've put a guard on Alex in case someone wants to off her, or worse."

"Thanks, Mike. We'll have to make a plan to ensure her safety until we can determine what this is all about."

"Now what?" Miss Maggie said as Irv disconnected.

"The Crescent City Police had to let the two suspects go."

There was a collective gasp and comments such as, "How can they do that?" and "There is no justice."

"She's in danger then," Miss Maggie stated emphatically.

"The Crescent City Police have a guard on her." Giving Miss Maggie a stern look, the chief said, "Miss Maggie, don't go getting any ideas about going over there."

"You spoil all my fun," she replied, disappointedly.

"If you want to keep Alex safe, leave it to the professionals. Thanks for the dinner."

The next morning, Chief Pauls boarded the six-a.m. *Golden Hind* for Crescent City. He was sure Alex would be able to talk, and he wanted to be there. On the hydrofoil, he called the chief of detectives, Mike Benton, to tell him he would be at the Crescent City dock at seven fifteen.

Detective Benton met him, and they drove to the hospital for breakfast. "Cathy has been in touch with the doctor caring for Alex, and by nine this morning, we should be able to talk with her."

"I hope she can identify those men and tell us what this is all about," the chief said.

Shortly after, as Chief Pauls and Mike Benton entered Alex's room, they saw that a nurse had carefully combed Alex's hair, but she still looked pale and tired. "Good morning, Alex," the chief said. "I hope we won't tire you out." Turning towards

Detective Benton, he added, "I know you know his wife, but have you met her husband, Detective Mike Benton?"

"I don't think so, but I'm glad to meet you."

"Alex, what was this all about?"

"Chief, I don't know. They kept telling me that they knew I had it and if I gave it to them, they would let me go. They would not tell me what 'it' was. I pretended to take them to it, took them to the dock, thinking I could swim away, but they were too quick for me. A boat with a fisherman was outside my channel, and I yelled at him, but I don't think he heard."

"You were lucky. The fisherman was your friend, Jason Hopkins, who heard and acted. He called us, said two men were with you, and that you had hollered for help."

"Thank heavens they ignored those men when they told him not to pay any attention to me, said I was crazy. I didn't know who it was and was sure I would be ignored."

"As you can see, Jason did not ignore you. He knows you're not crazy and would never joke like that."

"I owe him a lot of thanks. I think the plan was to take me off the island, find an isolated spot, and make me give them what they wanted, whatever that was." She paused and, in a frustrated manner, continued, "How could I give them something when I didn't know what it was?"

"Do you know either of them?"

"No. One of them came to the door and said he was Major somebody, Baxter, I think. Said I had taken care of him in Iraq, and he wanted to thank me personally. He handed me a dozen roses and asked if he could come in. I told him no, but that I would meet him at the Busted Jib. Then another guy popped up, and they both pushed their way in."

Chief Benton showed Alex a picture of each of them and asked, "Was it either of these men?"

"The tall one, the one who said he was a major, and the

other guy was the one who joined him when they pushed their way in. Did you catch them?

"We caught them but had to let them go."

"What?" Alex asked incredulously. "How could you let them go?"

"Lawyers and connections."

Alex closed her eyes and sighed. "Guess that explains the guard outside my door. You think they'll try again."

"Given what you are supposed to have, I think it is highly likely. Is there anything you have not told us? Do you have any idea what 'it' is?"

"No! Let alone where 'it' is."

"I think you need to go into hiding until we get this sorted out," Chief Pauls said.

"Stop being ridiculous. I'm safe on Rabbit Island. They need me at the Clinic."

Before either man could voice a disagreement, the doctor entered and suggested that Alex needed to rest. "We would like to send her home tomorrow, but she needs to be a little healthier before we can do that."

"Understand," Detective Benton said. "Alex, this is not the end of this discussion. My wife would be very upset with me if I let anything happen to you."

"See you tomorrow," the chief said. "And do as the doc says."

As they walked away, Chief Pauls told Mike, "Let's go somewhere private and discuss this."

"How about my office at the Station?"

"Fine."

Once there, Chief Pauls said, "I think I have a plan. Alex's good friend, Pete Harris, is, as you know, a celebrity of sorts. We will tell him that Alex needs a place to hide and see if he will hide her. From what I've heard via the grapevine, he has an estate surrounded by a high wrought iron fence, an electric fence inside, and a high hedge that provides privacy. I think we could keep her safe there. And, it's more likely she will be agreeable to this."

"That has possibilities." As Mike said this, an officer knocked on the door and said, "You have two visitors, FBI."

"Show them in." Turning to the chief, he said, "It looks like this is bigger than either of us thought yesterday. Although I'm not surprised, the lawyer, I'm sure, was from a cartel."

"Nor am I," the chief replied as two FBI agents entered.

"Glad we could see you. I'm Agent Andrew Caldwell, and with me is Agent Sherry Bowen."

Detective Benton acknowledged them and introduced the chief.

"Can you tell us what you know about your attempted kidnapping yesterday? We tried to talk to the victim, a Dr. Lawson, I believe, but were told that she needed to rest and that you two had just talked with her?"

Detective Benton shared with the two agents what he knew, including that Dr. Lawson, or Alex as she was known, did not know what it was about.

"We believe she needs protection," the Chief added. "Mike, Detective Benton, has placed a twenty-four-hour guard on her."

"We saw that." Agent Caldwell said. "Given that high-priced lawyer who hightailed it here by private plane from Detroit, that was a good idea."

The chief then outlined the plan he and Mike had discussed. "I think we could work with that. Will this Dr. Lawson go along with it? Victims can often discount their own danger."

"I will see that she does," the Chief said. "Meanwhile, I think she is safe here. Once they release her from the hospital, we'll take her home. The owner of Rabbit Island Air has agreed to come and get her, so she should be safe on the trip home. I will stay with her at her house, convince her to let us protect her, and then let her pack some things. We think she can be safe with an acquaintance of hers, Pete Harris."

"The TV star?"

"Yes."

"We will have to talk with him and have someone visit there before we can agree," Agent Caldwell said.

"I have no doubt he will agree and that you will find his home very suitable."

"Once we decide where she is going, it will be best if she does not even know where she is going. People don't mean to let things slip, but they often do."

"Understand. If you think this is a good idea, we'll need your help to get her secretly to Mr. Harris' home," Mike said.

"We were thinking of a safe house," Agent Bowen said.

"You are more likely to get Alex's cooperation if you use our plan," the chief said.

"I suppose it does have possibilities."

"Andrew, if Dr. Lawson is as spirited as we have heard, I think we should use their plan," Agent Bowen said.

"Sherry, are you a fan of Mr. Harris?"

"No, but being with Dr. Lawson will be easier if she cooperates."

"The other alternative is a safe house," Agent Caldwell replied. "But maybe these gentlemen have a good plan. I'll have it checked out." He turned to Agent Bowen and said, "If this works out, you can become her maid."

"I've had worse assignments."

Linda Q. Thede

16 Alex Goes to a Safe House

Alex was released from the hospital the next day with instructions not to go back to work for a few days. Mike escorted her to the Crescent City General heliport, where Tony and the chief picked her up. It was a short flight, and after they landed, the chief drove Alex to her home. There, Alex found another policeman, whom she did not know, and an unknown man and woman. Chief Pauls pointed to the policeman, "He will be your bodyguard until we can move you to a safe place."

"Bodyguard, safe place? What do you mean?"

"Alex, as you are aware, we had to let those two you identified as your abductors loose. They quickly lawyered up, and he got them out on a quarter of a million dollar bond each, even though no one had had a chance to talk with you. Makes me wonder if the judge they found had connections."

"Can't I just stay here and go to work? I don't want to go anywhere else. Dr. Gould needs me," she paused, adding emphatically. "I'm not going to leave!"

"Alex, did you even consider the danger you might be putting someone else in? Nora, the doctor, or your patients. Your abductors mean business. It would help, of course, if you knew what they wanted."

Alex was quiet as she considered what the chief had told her. "I hate to have them make me run scared. If they try again, won't my bodyguards catch them in the act?"

"I'm not certain enough to trust that would happen. Alex, this time, you were lucky. Another time, you might not be so lucky. The two individuals standing beside you are FBI agents. The man is Agent Caldwell, and the woman is Agent Bowen," Chief Pauls informed her. "Alex, you or anyone around you here is not safe. The FBI is working the case from their end and is arranging for you to go to safety."

"Where am I going?"

"To a safe house."

She laughed. "I never thought that would happen to me."

"Well, it has, and Agent Bowen here will be with you, acting as your maid," Agent Caldwell told her in a no-nonsense manner.

"I don't need a maid," Alex said defensively, "I can take care of myself."

"Yes, I'm sure you can, but we suspect you want to stay alive. As your maid, she can more easily protect you." Agent Caldwell paused to let that sink in. "As you said earlier, Dr. Gould and the island need you."

"Miss Maggie is going to have a cow when she doesn't know where I am."

"She'll have to live with that. But I'm sure she'll understand," Chief Pauls said.

"Can you at least give me a hint about how to pack? I assume I will get to do that."

"Think hot or cold and plan to layer."

How cold and how hot?"

"Moderate for both,"

"You're not much help." As she said that, her phone rang. "Miss Maggie," she said, looking at caller ID. "No doubt, a dinner invitation. Can I accept?"

"Yes, but Camille and I will come too."

"Hello, Miss Maggie."

"Alex, I'm so glad you're home. You must come for dinner tonight. I'd like you to stay with me until you're fully recovered. Minnie and I can keep you safe."

"Miss Maggie, dinner would be great, but Irv and Camille will be with me."

"Your protection, right?"

"Yes. The chief will have one of his officers stay here with me until this is cleared up."

"See you at five-thirty. Until then, get some rest."

Returning home after dinner at Miss Maggie's with the Police Chief and his wife, Alex was introduced to another officer who was to provide her security that night. "I hate to have you spend your night watching me for what is unlikely to happen. It makes me feel like a toddler, having to be watched."

"Not to worry, Dr. Lawson. I'm happy to be of service."

"Thank you. Help yourself to whatever food or drink you can find."

"No need for that. I came prepared." He showed Alex a thermos and lunch bucket."

She started up the spiral staircase to her room and told him, "Use the microwave if you need to. Good night." She still did not wholly accept her need for protection until her memory replayed the scene when the shorter intruder was told by the man posing as Major Baxter that he would have to wait to "persuade" Alex to give them what they wanted. The shorter intruder had then grinned evilly at her, got in her face, and said, "If you don't give it to us now, I'm going to make you wish you had never been born." And don't think you can die to get away. I'm far too experienced to lose a victim. It will be fun – for me." Then he smirked and whispered to her, "Don't tell, let me have my fun."

"Okay, Eduardo," the tall one had told him. "She's stubborn." He turned to Alex and said, "You will live to regret not giving us what we want."

"How can I give you something when I don't know what it is?" Alex stated, frustrated and scared.

"Have it your way, Dr. Lawson," the tall, dark man had said. "Eduardo, don't worry, you will get your chance. She wants to play dumb."

"I'm glad." Rubbing his hands together in anticipation, he added, "I can't wait."

Those memories quickened her step to her bedroom and her resolve to pack for her trip, wherever it might be. She wondered how long she would be there and decided to plan for an indefinite stay, even though she hoped it would not be very long. She threw a few things she would need on the sofa in her upstairs room, then started to pack. Taking a moment to consider what else to take, she looked at Lake Michigan, from which the reflection of the sunset had not yet entirely disappeared, a view that usually calmed her, but today, it looked as mixed up as she felt.

Alex was surprised when her phone rang early the next morning, and she was told her trip had been arranged. You are booked on the early afternoon flight to Chicago. At O'Hare, you need to make yourself noticed before you catch a plane to Houston. Get into a tiff with a salesperson at the bookstore, so if anyone is following you, they will be sure to notice."

"I thought I was supposed to be going into hiding. Why should I make myself noticed?"

"All part of the plan. We have arranged for Miss Maggie and the doctor to be at the airport to say goodbye. You are to loudly tell them you are going to Houston for a rest. A limo will meet you in Houston. Inside, you will change clothes with your double. The double will go to a 'safe house' and be seen going inside. Now dressed differently, you will be driven to Dallas to Love Field and board a plane to your safe place."

"It all sounds very complicated."

"It will work. Please, follow directions. We can only help you if you cooperate. Is that clear?"

"I guess so. I don't have much choice, do I?"

"Not if you want to live."

Much to her surprise, eight hours later, Pete greeted her with a big hug at his estate. "Just like you to make a big production of visiting me again. Couldn't stay away, eh?" He let her go and said, "You're a wonderful sight for a tired man. Perks me up." He kissed her. "By the way, this young woman is your maid, Sherry Bowen. I'm supposed to be a big, rich star; can't have a guest without a maid."

Embarrassed, Alex said, "A maid, I didn't have one last time I visited."

"Ah, but this time, I've been told you are here for the foreseeable future."

"Pete, are you saying I've been fobbed off on you to keep me safe?"

"Not fobbed off, placed here for safekeeping."

"I'm sorry, I would never willingly impose on you like this."

"Alex, don't worry, I'm delighted. However, we won't be able to do anything outside my house. I hope you won't be bored."

"I'd better be glad I'm here and not in some stuffy safe house somewhere. I enjoyed being here a while ago, and it's best that I set my mind to enjoying it now. Maybe I can use the time to write that article I want to submit to a nursing journal." She had brought her computer thinking she could put her time in 'jail,' as she couldn't help thinking of her stay, to good use. "You do have the Internet, yes?"

"Of course, and I have written down the password for you. You'll find it on the desk in your room." He turned to Sherry. "Would you take Dr. Lawson's things to her room and unpack for her? I want to show her around the place."

"Certainly, Mr. Harris."

"Alex, I hope we'll have some time for one another. If not for the circumstances, I would be overjoyed to have you here. I was lonely after you left. My biggest regret, however, is that we are still filming next year's shows and I'm busier than I like." As Pete told her this, he led Alex to a window where she could see the pool. "The pool," he continued, "is protected from prying eyes, so feel free to use it. I assume you brought your bathing suit. Although this is my busy season, I hope to join you for a swim now and then."

He directed her to her room and told her, "I imagine you've had a hard day and are tired. You remember Alice, my cook. She has fixed some sandwiches and soup for you. Freshen up and come down to the dining room."

"I hope I can find my way," Alex said.

"If you're as smart as I remember, you won't have forgotten," he told her.

Alex looked around her room, the same one she had occupied on her first visit. She saw that her things had been unpacked and heard a knock on her door. "Come in."

"Dr. Lawson, I feel you are uncomfortable with a maid. I may be more experienced in my role than you are in yours."

"Amen. Thank you for unpacking for me."

"Just part of the job. My room is next to you and has a listening device. I can hear anything happening here. And no, you don't have much privacy, but rest assured, I don't tell, and I can be here in a flash if needed. We aim to keep you safe until we can untangle this mess."

"Like coming here, I didn't have many options, did I?"

"Afraid not."

"No reason why we can't be friends, is there? I'd love to hear more about your work."

"It's a lot duller than you think."

"Let's hope it stays that way until we are out of this. I have to keep telling myself to have patience."

"I understand. For now, take Mr. Harris's advice, freshen up, and get something to eat."

"Will you have something with us?"

"Of course not. The help eats in the kitchen, but do not worry. The fare there is as excellent as what you'll get. And I've already eaten."

Alice's sandwiches and soup went down easily. "I'm glad you like them," Pete told her. "But then, Alice is a great cook."

"Thank her for me. Pete, I'm drained."

"I'm not surprised." He got up and looked at Alex, saying, "I'll take you to your room."

Despite the stress of the day and the uncertainty and sadness of leaving Rabbit Island and her job, Alex fell asleep shortly after pulling the covers around her. The next morning, the filtered light of a sunbeam flashing through the trees around her room awakened her. Sitting up with a start, she said, "Where am I?" Then it all came back, and she sighed and lay back down. A knock on her door told her that Agent Bowen was already up and ready to play her maid role.

"Come in."

"I heard you stirring and heard you ask where you were—not surprised. That sometimes happens to me in a strange place. If it's okay with you, I'll tell the cook you are up and tell her to prepare a tray."

"Won't I be eating with Pete?"

"He was out of here at five this morning. Making a show is not all glamor, but early mornings and often late nights. If you like, perhaps we can bend the rules, and I will eat with you. You can say you don't want to eat alone and ask me to join you."

"I'd like company. This role of spoiled brat is not fun."

Agent Bowen laughed. "Relax and enjoy it. This is easy work for me. And the quick change yesterday went well. It looks like you are safe."

"Glad to hear you say it."

Determined to make the best of her situation, after getting dressed and enjoying breakfast with Sherry, Alex started reading the book she had bought at the airport in Chicago when she created a scene to make herself visible. After lunch, she decided to go for a swim. She asked Sherry to join her, but was told maids don't swim with their mistresses. What a crock, she thought. But she could not fight it.

Pete arrived home at about seven, and Alex was able to have dinner with him, but it was apparent he was tired. "Tough day on the set?"

"You said it. The director was in a bad mood, and the actress playing the femme fatale did not know her lines. He was disgusted and said she'd never work with him again. But enough of me. How was your day?"

"I did some reading and went swimming."

"Did you start writing your article?"

"Did a little research and jotted down some ideas and references."

"I hope your room is okay. I hate not being able to be a good host. Perhaps Sunday. If we have this week's episode in the can."

"Pete, don't worry about me. I'm safe here, and that is what counts. You are not obligated to play host."

"I don't feel obligated. I want to. And I feel I'm missing the opportunity for us to continue renewing our old acquaintance. We were pretty good together then, yes?" he stated, putting his arm around her and pulling her closer.

She smiled and felt comforted, "Yes, we were."

Embracing her, he kissed her. She responded, more from habit than the electricity of old.

Pete did have Sunday off, and as promised, they spent the day together, swimming and racing in the pool as they had done on her earlier visit and as they used to when they were younger and more carefree—neither noticed a quiet drone that watched them enjoy themselves.

After their swim, Pete asked her to help him learn his lines for next week's filming. Surprisingly, she found it fun to try to get into the role of the different characters the script called for him to interact with.

"You missed your calling. You should have been an actress."

"You do know how to lather it on, don't you? But thanks for the compliment. Anyhow, I'm happy being a nurse practitioner."

"Don't sell yourself short. If I didn't have to keep you hidden, I would have you replace that dumb broad who keeps muffing her lines. A rock would beat her in intelligence. All she has going for her is her looks. At least she won't be in the show again. The director and I will see to that."

"You think that slowed up production? How about an amateur cluttering up the scene?"

"I remember you and me working together in a play in high school."

"I remember. One afternoon, I completely forgot my lines. Fortunately, you rescued me."

"But that was in the dress rehearsal. You were perfect in our two shows."

"Ah, those days."

"How are you coming with your article?"

"I've made a stab at it. The research is done, and now I'm working on the organization. Have maybe a paragraph or two written. And I finished the book I bought at the Chicago airport."

"So that's what prevented you from writing."

"Guilty as charged. I've promised myself that I will explore the books in your library when the article is done. That's the gold at the end of my rainbow." She paused, smiled, and added, "That was another thing we shared, a love of reading. Although our tastes in books were not always the same. But after I outgrew Nancy Drew, I enjoyed some of yours."

"Promise me you'll finish writing this week."

"I can't promise. Sometimes, I run into a snag when the information I need is not easily available. Fortunately, I can still access journals online. I never gave up my association with the University of Michigan."

"Early day tomorrow," Pete said, helping her to her feet, hugging her, and kissing her goodnight. "See you sometime."

17 FEDERICO'S & EDUARDO'S DEMISE

While Alex and Pete were saying goodnight, Federico called Javier. "I know where she is."

"How did you find her?"

"Before we left her house, I got her cell phone number. After we were released, I used it to follow her. I heard the local gossip about her and Pete Harris, and found her at his house. A few days after she arrived, I had a drone pass over the estate and take pictures as she and Pete were swimming. When I looked at the films, I identified her."

"Okay, now get that thumb drive."

"We will, don't worry."

Unaware that she had been identified, Alex resolved to try to finish or at least get most of her article written. She wrote two pages, then became lost in thought. Hoping to find a solution, she fingered her computer case. "What is this?" she said aloud as her fingers found something hard in a compartment in her computer case. She pulled a thumb drive out. "I don't remember putting this in here. What on earth did I put on it before putting it here?"

Sherry, watching her, said, "You could put it in your computer and find out."

"You mean be smart." Laughing, she inserted it into the computer. Looking at the file names, she realized they were all spreadsheet files. She opened one of the files and saw a column of names, kilograms, and places. "Sherry, look at this. What do you think it is?"

Looking at the files, Sherry said, "I think this may be why you were abducted and what the 'it' is. To me, it looks like a record of narcotics exchanges filed with the location where they were picked up or distributed from."

"How did I get it?"

"That only you can answer. But I am fairly certain this is what all this is about."

Alex shook her head. "Thumb drives don't grow on trees. Where did it come from?"

"You'll have to figure that out, but I know where it's going." Saying that Sherry called the local FBI office and asked them to send some agents out to get the drive.

"Will this get me out of hiding?" Alex asked.

"I don't know. The people who wanted this drive may want to punish you. And you haven't explained how you got it."

Moaning, Alex said, "I'll be here forever."

"Don't get discouraged so easily."

Five minutes later, Sherry said, "Someone is knocking on the front door. I didn't think they could get here this quickly. They must have been in the area. Maybe checking on us." With that, she ran downstairs and started to open the door. When it was partially opened, two men dressed in suits pushed in. "We're FBI agents. I understand you have an Alexandra Lawson here. We want to talk to her."

"Let me see your identification."

"We don't have time for that. We need to retrieve something that she should not have. Where is it?"

"I have no idea, either what it is or where it is," Sherry lied, recognizing them as Alex's abductors. "And neither does she."

One of the men took out a gun and pointed it at Sherry, "Quit stalling. You have ten seconds to take us to her, one, two."

She led the men to Alex's room as the man kept counting. "In there," Sherry said, pointing to Alex's room and trying to stay back." Grabbing Sherry around the neck with one arm and with the other, holding his gun against Sherry's head, they burst into Alex's room.

Federico saw the drive protruding from Alex's computer, "Give me that drive!"

Recognizing the two men as the ones who tried to kidnap her, Alex hesitated, shut down her computer, pulled the drive out, and started to get up to give it to Federico. Instead, she quickly turned to the open window and threw it out. "Go get it!"

Angry, the tall man slapped her hard and said, "Lady, if I were not in such a hurry, you'd pay for this. As would this broad," he said roughly, hurling Sherry away from him. He turned to Eduardo, "We have to get that drive and get out of here." They hurried down the stairs and outside before Alex or Sherry could react.

As Federico retrieved the drive from the hedge, Alex and Sherry heard through the window, "All right, gentlemen, that's enough. Get your hands up! You," he said, pointing a gun at Federico, who had picked up the drive. "Drop it."

Federico pushed the business end of the drive out, then dropped it and smashed that end hard with his heel while pretending to lose his balance. Pointing to it, he said pleasantly, "Put your guns away. Why the interest? It's just a thumb drive. You can pick it up. We're leaving."

"Not so fast."

"What is this? A dictatorship? You can't hold me here."

Watching through the window, Sherry rushed downstairs and joined the two men who had stopped Alex's abductors from taking the drive. "Thank goodness you're here." She pointed at the two perpetrators, "These two men said they were FBI agents, held me hostage, and attempted to take that drive from Dr. Lawson." Hearing that, the two men started to dash for the gate. They were, however, no match for the two FBI agents and soon were in their custody.

As the other agent called for backup, one of the men showed Sherry his FBI identification and asked her, "What was on this drive that made it so important?"

"It looked like data about drug deals," Sherry told them.

As the two were being led away, Sherry and the FBI agents entered the house. Alex, one side of her face red from the slap, greeted them after they entered the house.

"What happened to you?" one of the agents asked.

"One of those men slapped her hard when she threw the drive out the window," Sherry told them.

One of the FBI agents held up the damaged drive, "We'll have to see if the lab can decipher anything on this."

"You won't need to do that. When I heard those men downstairs with Sherry, I copied the files to my computer. I was lucky to finish just before they entered the room."

"Good thinking."

"These people have wreaked havoc on my life. Because of them, I've been in jail. I want to go home."

The FBI agents exchanged looks. "Alex," Sherry asked, "don't you think we need to find out who 'these people' are before someone connected with them wants to take revenge?"

"Sherry, they think the drive is destroyed and the data gone. They won't waste time trying to get back at me."

"Dr. Lawson, we are dealing with a rather bad bunch. Are you sure they will believe the drive was destroyed? And be sure that no one can get anything from it? The group may be small now, but they are trying to grow. In Boston, in a fight for territory, they left several dead bodies. Do you want to be one of those?"

Alex shook her head and sighed. "So, I'm still in jail."

"Ma'am, I don't think you'll ever find a jail as nice as this," the other agent said.

"But now they know where I am. You'll have to move me."

"Possibly. But we'd like to talk to Mr. Harris. With the addition of a few dogs and other security measures, you would be safe here, and we might be able to flush more of them out when we pretend to move you. These two will not be released like they were after they abducted you."

"Pete's going to love that. Right in the middle of filming for the season. You'll have to imprison him too. They could use him to get to me."

"There is no reason for anyone to know you are still here. We will stage your departure with your look-alike in a somewhat sloppy manner so that, if interested, they will follow. So, Mr. Harris can go on as before. But there will be security, invisible to most eyes, but, nonetheless, here. Much more than we had before."

"Am I now a decoy?"

"I suppose so until we can arrange your supposed 'move.' How else can we make you safe?"

"You can start by getting that data off my computer and cleaning it so there is no history of the data ever being there."

"I've arranged for someone to do that later today. By the way, do you have your cell phone with you?"

"Yes, but I have it turned off."

"Unfortunately, it still leaves a trail. We should have taken it away and given it to your decoy. Until we can arrange your 'move,' we will leave it with you. But it will go with your decoy."

Alex sighed. "Technology turned upside down. I'm tired of all this Mickey Mouse." Not happy, she mumbled under her breath, "Just more intrigue." Out loud, she asked, "Sherry, can you tell the cook we'd all like some lunch?"

"No need, Ma'am, I figured that out," Alice, the cook, said, placing a plate of sandwiches on the table where a tureen of soup stood. After lunch, the two local agents left, and Alex sought out Alice.

"Alice, that was delicious. I bet those two agents never had it so good. Many thanks."

"Dr. Lawson, I was happy to do it." Smiling, she added, "I could see that they enjoyed it. That was payment enough."

That evening, when Pete arrived home, Alex rushed to meet him and tell him what had happened. He laughed. "Why am I filming make-believe when the real thing is happening in my own home?" He kissed her. "I know all about it. The FBI interrupted the entire set to tell the story."

"Oh, Pete, I'm so sorry."

"I'm glad that we finally know what "it" is. And that you can continue to stay here. The agents took me aside and proposed to step up security at my place and keep you here."

"After this mess, you still want me to stay here?"

"I don't want it any other way. Join me now for supper. Then later, you can help me with my lines."

The next day, Alex's charade of leaving Pete's house was performed to perfection. If only I could change places with my double, she thought. I've got 'house fever.' As lovely as Pete's house is, it's still confining.

The thumb drive gone, life went back to what it had been. Two days later, Alex finished the first draft of her article about practicing as a nurse practitioner on an island. "Now to do an edit for obvious things, then put it aside for a while so I can recognize where I've gone wrong."

A few days later, the two FBI agents who had taken the data from Alex's computer were at the door. Sherry let them in, asking, "What's happening?"

"Get Dr. Lawson, she needs to hear this. And don't worry, it's not bad news."

When Alex entered the room, one of the agents said, "Dr. Lawson, welcome to freedom. Those two who wanted that drive collapsed under pressure and told us everything. They were not high up in the organization, but with their knowledge and the data on the drive, we've been able to break up the entire cartel. It was pretty small as cartels go, but you are now safe. There is no one left to come after you. And it seems your missing passenger on that flight from Honolulu to Chicago was part of their group."

"Could he have put that thumb drive in my computer case? While I was occupied with Miss Maggie and her great-niece, I left the case on the seat between us. I noticed when I returned that he seemed calmer than when I left."

"It would explain how it came to be there," the FBI agent said.

"When will you be leaving?" Sherry asked.

"As soon as I can. Tomorrow, if possible. I'm going to look into a ticket now. She left the FBI agents and used her phone to buy tickets. However, it was not until the following Tuesday that Alex could obtain a ticket to Rabbit Island.

She returned to the group. "I can't get home until Tuesday. However, that day, I have an early morning flight to Chicago and a connecting flight to Rabbit Island. Now, I want to let Miss Maggie know." Laughing, she said, "I bet she's been driving Chief Pauls crazy asking where I am."

Sherry looked at Alex. "Sorry you can't go home any sooner. But how would you like to go shopping this afternoon?"

"A wonderful idea. I want out!!!" As an afterthought, she added, "Sherry, does this mean you can't be my maid anymore?"

"I suspect so."

Alex laughed, "How on earth am I expected to manage without a maid?"

"I think you'll figure it out." She laughed. "You never learned how to use one. And I think the agency will allow us an afternoon out before I'm reassigned."

Enjoying her first taste of freedom, Alex and Sherry selected Rodeo Drive for their expedition. They did more window shopping than anything else. Prices on Rodeo Drive are, Alex thought, way out of line. They arrived home and found Pete waiting for them. "Oh, Pete, I have the most wonderful news."

"I know, an agent dropped by the set to tell me. I'm happy for you." He smiled slyly. "And I have news for you. There is a small part in the show we're filming next week that I'd like you to play."

"Come on, Pete, I want to go home. I have a ticket for Tuesday."

"We'll film it on Monday. And this weekend, we'll swim without being observed by drones, then rehearse.

"Pete, this is silly. I'm an amateur. I'll just clutter up your set."

"Alex, let me worry about that. I did you a favor. Now it's your turn to do me one. And Saturday night, I'm taking you to a party."

"I don't have anything to wear."

Pete laughed. "All afternoon shopping, and you can say that. Not to worry, it's very casual."

"Where is it?"

"At one of my friend's homes."

"Who will be there?"

"You'll have to wait to find out."

Alex hoped she would not embarrass herself. She did not keep up with Hollywood glitterati and probably would not recognize anyone. Saturday evening, she dressed in what she thought were her best casual clothes, wearing her white slacks with the one top she had splurged on in her shopping spree.

Descending the stairs after finishing dressing, Pete looked at her and whistled. "You look dazzling. I'll be the envy of all at the party."

18 ALEX'S INTRODUCTION TO SHOW BUSINESS

Despite dressing carefully for the party that Pete was taking her to, Alex was uneasy. She was afraid she would not fit in. She was surprised to find the party was at Brittany Prince's. She had not seen her since the night Brittany embarrassed her at Steve's Island Resort.

Walking into the party, over the music, she heard Brittany say, "Welcome, Dr. Lawson and Pete."

"Please call me Alex. I only use doctor professionally."

"As you wish." Pointing to a bar and table laden with food, Brittany said, "Go help yourself. " Then she turned away and walked towards a tall, blonde man who put his arm around her as they went to talk to some of the other guests.

Pete led her to the bar and ordered her a vodka tonic and himself a Scotch on ice. While waiting for their drinks, another woman approached, saying, "Pete, this is who you've been hiding. Introduce me."

"Karen, this is Alex Lawson, star of cartel-busting."

Karen extended her hand. "Welcome, Alex. After exchanging pleasantries, Karen said, "I hear you outdid Pete here in the excitement phase."

"Not by choice. But that is behind me."

"Karen, introduce me," a man joining Karen said.

"Alex, meet Jeff."

"Pete, you old fox. I see why you kept her hidden. Now,

Alex, may I have this dance?"

Alex looked at Pete, who motioned for her to accept.

"You're new to this scene, aren't you?"

"Is it that obvious?"

"I sense a little unease. We may seem different to someone unaccustomed to meeting show business folks, but underneath, we are just like everyone else. With just as many doubts about ourselves, maybe more."

"I have to confess, I don't read the gossip magazines, and outside of Pete, Brittany, you, and Karen, whom I've just met, I don't have the foggiest idea who anyone is."

"We're not all famous. There are quite a few hangers-on here. Brittany loves introducing new talent to others. She remembers how she got her start. Now, I'd better return you to Pete, or he may get upset."

Glancing at Pete, Alex was sure he was looking jealously at Brittany. She wondered if he wanted to repair their relationship. Was she just a token to make Brittany jealous? Despite the fun they had enjoyed the past few weeks, she felt Pete was holding back and playing the role expected of him.

As Jeff delivered her to Pete, she saw him quickly turn away from watching Brittany. "Let's dance. I've been standing here, jealous of Jeff." As they danced, Alex felt he was employing his acting skills as he made a show of being delighted to be with her. Dancing to place them near Brittany at the end of the dance, he hugged her and said, "That was wonderful." He kissed her and then glanced at Brittany to see her reaction. Surprisingly, Alex thought she saw a hint of jealousy in Brittany, like she had displayed when singing You Ain't Woman Enough to Take My Man to her.

Later that evening, on their way home, Pete seemed to force himself to be romantic. In a voice lacking enthusiasm, he said. "No bodyguard, you can now enjoy spending the night in my room."

"Pete, I'm too tired. Let's just call it a night."

Pete appeared relieved. "I understand." He gave her a friendly kiss on the cheek. "See you tomorrow."

Turning the evening events over in her mind, Alex was sure Pete was still in love with Brittany. She wondered if she was one of the reasons for their breakup. Truthfully, she had to admit she wasn't serious about Pete either. It was flattering to think a TV star found her attractive, but she was afraid she was using him to try to make Tony jealous. A waste of effort, she concluded. If he wants that Gina, he's entitled to her. I'll stay out of the picture. I don't need a man. I have a good life on Rabbit Island, a lovely home, and am fixed financially with my Air Force pension, the income from the investments Dad made with my savings and a regular salary. She laughed. "I'm what any man would want, a nurse with a purse." But then she remembered she was through with men.

She and Pete spent Sunday as the friends they were, but not as two people romantically involved. They raced again in the pool and laughed as they sunned themselves. "That's a nice tan you'll take home. But you always did tan easily. And it looks good on you."

Later that day, they rehearsed the scene he had prevailed on her to do. It was a small but essential part. Her character only appeared once but was an important part of the story. Besides helping her with her lines, he acted as a director and guided her in the motions and positions she needed to depict the character. "You're ready, Alex. Now, get a good night's sleep. It's a five o'clock morning."

Monday morning, Pete ushered her onto the set, introduced her, and took her to a dressing room where a hairdresser was waiting. After her hair was done, the makeup artist visited. Then it was wait with all the butterflies in the world playing hopscotch in her stomach. Despite her nervousness, she managed to eat a little soup for lunch. Finally, at two, she was called to the set. Working hard to try and stay calm, she reminded herself that the rehearsal with Pete the day before had gone well. But a voice kept telling her this was the real thing.

Pete greeted her with a hug. "Okay, Alex, break a leg."

After some instruction, blocking, she thought they called it, and the cameras ready, she heard, "Scene 3, take one," and the red light turned on. Surprising herself, she remembered her lines and the motions with them. Pete was easy to work with, and he led her when necessary, letting her shine during her part. When it was over, the director said, "Okay, we don't need any more takes. Dr. Lawson, you can leave if you wish. He looked at Pete and smiled. "Or, wait for him."

That evening at home, Pete was all smiles. "Alex, you were terrific. There are more parts for you if you will do them."

"Pete, I'm not ready for your life. And I want to get back to Rabbit Island. I'm very grateful to you. But I want to get back to normal."

"If you insist, but expect me to ask you to do more parts on the show. Meanwhile, how about one last glass of wine together before you leave tomorrow?"

"Certainly," she said and smiled. Later, as they parted, Alex thought about the day's events as she prepared to spend her last night at Pete's. She realized that much to her surprise, she had enjoyed acting with Pete. She had not had to interact with any of the other actors, who might not have given her the support Pete had. She also wondered if the fact that there was only one take meant the director had decided to cut the scene and use dialot to characterize the character. Oh well, she had had fun.

She missed Sherry. She had had to say goodbye to her Saturday morning when she left for her home, where she was promised some free time to enjoy her family. They had become very friendly, and Alex hoped they might see each other again, but as the friends they had become, not as protector and "protectee."

Was Tony jealous now that he knew where she had been? Probably not. It was time to get on with her life. Alex strongly suspected that Gina was jealous because she believed Alex had immediately found someone else and that someone was famous. She was sure that given a chance for someone she considered a 'better catch,' Gina would dump Tony. Gina was built with the green-eyed monster.

She doubted that Gina truly loved Tony, but that was his problem. She refused to make it hers. Laughing to herself, she thought, wait until she finds out I will be in one of Pete's shows. She decided, however, that until she knew her scene had not ended up on the cutting room floor, she would keep this a secret. If it stays in, I can spring it then.

Although Alex was glad to be going home, the next morning she found it bittersweet to say goodbye to Pete. He had been a wonderful host, and she knew he was a true friend. She was, however, sure he was still in love with Brittany and was afraid she was not free of Tony. In her opinion, forming a relationship with someone else when one was not mentally free was deceitful. Although she and Pete had warm feelings for each other, it was more like a brother-sister relationship. As the novelty of reconnecting wore off, they realized they lived in different worlds and were happy in their worlds. She suspected that his show Saturday night of being romantically involved with her was to make Brittany jealous. She hoped it had worked.

Her seven AM flight to Chicago took off and arrived on time. In the waiting room at O'Hare, Alex was surprised to hear, "Colonel Lawson!"

Turning towards the voice, she recognized Dr. Norse,

who still thought of her as the Air Force Colonel she was when they met in Iraq. Surprised, she asked, "What are you doing here?"

"The same thing you are, waiting for the flight to Rabbit Island. However, I'm going on to Traverse City for a conference. But I'm returning to Rabbit Island on Friday, and my wife is joining me. We're spending the weekend at Steve's Island Resort. Nadia and her mother have told us a lot about the island, and we look forward to visiting. My hidden reason for visiting is to check up on Mrs. Duliami. But I also want to see Rabbit Island, where it's still nice outside in mid-November! Wish I could say the same for Chicago."

"Rabbit Island does have its quirks. I hope we have a good weekend for you."

"We've been promised a suite with a lake view. It will be interesting to be on the east side of Lake Michigan instead of the west. I hope we'll get some wonderful sunsets."

The loudspeaker announced the Blue Water flight, and Alex joined Dr. Norse and the others in boarding the plane. As the flight gained altitude, Alex looked down at Lake Michigan, so blue in the noonday sun. Impatient for the flight to be over, she did not appreciate it as she usually did. Miss Maggie had told her she would be at the airport to greet her. She was lucky to have friends and support waiting for her. Maybe she would settle down on Rabbit Island permanently, even without Tony. She especially wanted to get back to work.

As the flight approached Rabbit Island, Alex could feel herself getting more and more excited. When the plane finally finished taxing and stopped near the gate, she thought they'd never get the stairs rolled over to the plane. Rabbit Island Airport had not yet installed jetways, although Alex knew they were on Tony's list of desired improvements. The door finally opened, and she waved goodbye to Dr. Norse as she stood up to follow the line to deplane. Three-quarters of the way down the stairs, she felt a push from behind, lost her balance, and tumbled down the stairs, nearly knocking over the man in front of her, who tightly grabbed the railing and managed to stay upright as Alex nose-dived past him. Seeing her on the tarmac, the man she had almost knocked over stopped when his foot touched the ground and rushed to her as she lay on the tarmac.

"Let me help you up."

"No, let me be. I need to get myself together." Her neck hurt, and she felt numbness and weakness in her arms and legs and was afraid she would stumble if she tried to get up.

"Leave her be until we make sure we won't injure her further," a voice belonging to Dr. Norse carried over the crowd. He had been watching from the plane window, seen what happened, and quickly deplaned. He approached Alex, knelt down on the tarmac, and said, "Alex, where do you hurt?"

"My neck and upper back. Don't move me."

Looking over the crowd, Dr. Norse gestured to a ramp agent and said, "We'll need a neck collar and a backboard before moving her. She may have ruptured a few vertebrae. We cannot take any chances."

"But sir, we need to get this plane out of here. Can't we just pick her up and move her?"

"Young man, get me what I need. There is a life in the balance."

Seeing Alex lying on the tarmac, Miss Maggie, with her persuasive, some would say arrogant manner, had forced her way onto the field and to Alex. Hearing Dr. Norse say that Alex might have fractured one or more vertebrae, she called Rabbit Island Air and said they would need the chopper for Alex over at the airport. Then, she called the police and requested an ambulance as the ramp agent returned with the requested items. "I've ordered an ambulance to get Dr. Lawson over to where our helicopter can pick her up," she told Dr. Norse as he was helping the ramp agent put a neck collar and back brace on Alex.

When they finished, Dr. Norse said, "I'm taking the Colonel back to Northwestern to take care of her."

When the ambulance arrived, the attendant lowered a gurney and helped Dr. Norse load Alex on it. The pilot, Gina, supervised loading Alex into the helicopter, then told Miss Maggie and Dr. Norse, "She'll be okay. I'll take her to Crescent City General. Your work here is done.

"I think she may have ruptured a few vertebrae, and I want to take care of her. We need to go to Northwestern in Chicago."

Looking at Dr. Norse, Gina said, "We don't go there. Alex, you don't need to go to Chicago. I am taking you to Crescent City General. They can handle this. They don't need a black doctor telling them or me what to do. You are going to Crescent City General. You're not directing this show. I am."

"Gina, what is happening?" Alex heard Tony, who had been in another part of the airport but heard the commotion, ask over the noise of the idling helicopter.

"This crazy woman and black man think we should take Dr. Lawson to Chicago instead of Crescent City General or Downstate. And she wants this man," pointing to Dr. Norse, "to care for her."

Alex, her eyes cold, glared at Gina. "Gina, you are talking about Dr. Norse, one of the finest neurosurgeons in the country. If you or Tony won't take me there, I'm sure Dr. Norse can have Northwestern send us one of their helicopters."

Tony planted his feet firmly on the tarmac. "Alex, relax. I will take you, Miss Maggie, and Dr. Norse, to Northwestern. Gina, you return to the office and finish the reports you were working on.

Within the hour, they were at the Northwestern Heliport and met by some of Dr. Norse's team. "Let's get this patient into an examination room and alert radiology that I may need a CT scan," Dr. Norse told them. He turned to Miss Maggie. "I assume you'd like to stay with her."

After a complete neurological exam, Dr. Norse sent Alex for a CT scan. While he waited for the results, Miss Maggie asked, "Dr., how bad is it?"

"I suspect there may be two fractures of adjoining cervical vertebrae, but so far, I don't think there is permanent spinal cord injury. But there may be some swelling that could be creating the weakness in her arms and legs." He smiled at the concerned Miss Maggie. "I think she will be okay." Shortly, they were notified that the CT scan results were available.

After studying them, Dr. Norse said to Miss Maggie while Alex was wheeled back into the exam room, "A few bone fragments have escaped. I want to do surgery to clear those out and make sure nothing is pressing on the cord."

He approached Alex and said, "Colonel, you have some loose bone segments. They are minimal, but I want to do surgery to remove them."

"Dr. Norse, I trust you. Whatever you think is necessary, please do." She looked at Miss Maggie. "Thanks for coming with me. You'd better go back with Tony. I'll be fine here."

Miss Maggie emphatically told Alex, "Tony will wait for me if he knows what's good for him." She turned to Dr. Norse. "How long will the surgery take, and where can we wait?"

"I won't know until I get in there. We're lucky. There is a free operating room, and we can use it." As they were wheeling Alex away, he turned to Miss Maggie. "This nurse will show you where you can wait."

Once she knew where she would be waiting, Miss Maggie called Tony and told him that Alex was on her way to surgery, and he should return to Rabbit Island.

"No. I'm going to wait with you."

"Thanks, Tony. I'm in the surgical waiting room. Can you find it?"

"Of course. After I park the bird, I'll meet you there."

19 Northwestern University Hospital

Several hours after Tony had joined Miss Maggie in the surgical waiting room, a nurse took them to the recovery room. Greeting Alex, Miss Maggie said, "Alex, wake up. Your surgery is over. You are in the recovery room."

Alex opened her eyes, said, "Hello," and then closed them.

Dr. Norse entered as she and Tony found chairs near Alex. "Colonel, I was correct. There were a few bone fragments, but we took care of them. You won't miss them because they are not from a vital part of your cervical vertebrae. I expect a full recovery, but it will not be tomorrow, next week, or even next month. We will keep you here for a week. Once we release you, you will need rehab."

Weakly, Alex answered, "Understood."

"She can rehab with me," Miss Maggie said.

"A week or two of concentrated professional rehab would be better. After we are satisfied that the colonel is progressing well, we could consider sending her to you. I do not want her to live alone for at least three months. And she must keep up the exercises we will give her when we discharge her." He studied Miss Maggie, "I have a feeling that once she is with you, she will follow through."

Tony laughed. "I see you've already seen through our Miss Maggie."

Dr. Norse chuckled and looked at Miss Maggie. "And

appreciated her concern for the colonel. Captain Hamilton, thank you for bringing Colonel Lawson here. We worked together in Iraq for a short while. She taught me a few things, too. She was the nightmare of one of the other physicians, who was half-hearted in his work and spent time berating the nurses. That was something the colonel would not tolerate." He smiled at Miss Maggie, "A little like you when your feathers are ruffled. And tough as a bulldog."

"How long will she be in recovery?" Miss Maggie asked.

"Until her breathing, heart rate, and blood pressure have convinced me she can go to ICU. And she is a little less groggy. I will stay in town with her until Thursday. If I am certain she is okay, I will leave her with my team and go to Traverse City for my conference, then spend the weekend with my wife on Rabbit Island. "Why don't you two get something to eat in the cafeteria? It will probably be about an hour before we are comfortable transferring her."

As the trio left Alex's bedside, Tony said, "Dr. Norse, I will personally fly over and take you to Traverse City."

"That's very nice of you, but I am happy with Blue Water Air. But if I can't get a flight, I'll call you. Now, I'm going to show you where the cafeteria is."

After enjoying a hamburger in the hospital cafeteria, which Miss Maggie and Tony found surprisingly good, they arrived in the ICU shortly after Alex. Now more awake and connected to all the gadgets needed to monitor her condition, she greeted them both. "Where is my luggage and stuff that I had with me?"

"It's at your house," Tony said.

"Where's my cell phone?"

"I'm afraid it's still on Rabbit Island. The FBI returned it. I understand the kidnappers used it to track you, but now it's okay. Bill has a charter to Rockford, Illinois, tomorrow. He will arrange for it to be delivered to you."

"When you return to Rabbit Island, can one of you use my cell phone to call Pete? He's probably still on the set, but he gets home about six Pacific time, nine ours. I planned to call him this evening but don't have my phone."

"I will take care of it," Miss Maggie said.

"And for heaven's sake, don't worry him. He's got enough on his plate right now. I don't need him dropping everything and rushing out here."

"I'll tell him you are just as feisty as ever," Miss Maggie said with a broad grin.

"Folks, this patient needs her rest. You need to leave," they heard a nurse say.

As they stood up, Alex reached out and touched Miss Maggie's arm, smiled, and said groggily, "Thanks, both of you, for coming with me. I'll be okay now, but Rabbit Island needs you both."

Thursday afternoon, Dr. Norse felt that Alex had improved enough that he could attend his conference. "I'll be back Monday morning. I have left orders that if you are stable, then on Saturday, they should transfer you out of the ICU to a regular bed. This, of course, depends on you behaving. I expect to hear that you have behaved."

Alex, mindful of her neck collar, mimicked a salute. "Yes, sir." She paused, "I want to get better. I can't thank you enough for interrupting your vacation/conference to take care of me. I knew that if I needed neurosurgery, you were the only one I wanted to do it. I have watched you operate and envied you your skill."

"Colonel, I learned some things from you about observing patients that have helped me in my work. Just a little repayment."

"Have a good presentation, and enjoy your weekend on Rabbit Island. I wish I could be there to welcome you. But I'm sure Miss Maggie will take care of that."

He laughed. "A real hurricane, isn't she? I'm still amazed she could get through security and onto the tarmac after you fell."

"Miss Maggie generally gets her way, maybe because people know her and know she wants only the best for Rabbit Island. But you are right. She can be a hurricane." Alex said laughingly.

"Alex, you obey the nurses and doctors while I'm gone. If you do okay on the regular floor, we should be able to release you to our rehab center by Wednesday."

"When can I go back to Rabbit Island? And to work?"

"Easy there. Colonel, one must walk before one runs. Seriously, it's too early to tell, but you are still young and healthy. I expect to send you back to Rabbit Island in a couple of weeks. Will that Captain Hamilton come and get you?"

"I have no idea."

"I think he's sweet on you."

"No, he's with that pilot who was not going to take me here."

"Don't be so sure. Take care, and don't think you can get up and help."

Alex laughed, "Only when the spirit moves me." She paused and looked at him. "Seriously, I can be a good patient when necessary."

"It's necessary."

The next morning, as Alex was enjoying her coffee in her hospital bed, the name Pete Harris appeared in the ID of her phone as it rang.

"Alex, I've been so worried about you. Since Miss Maggie called me the day you left and told me what happened, I've been trying to reach you, but no one answered your phone."

"I was in ICU for a few days, and even after being transferred, I haven't felt up to talking to anyone until now."

"I'm going to come out and see you this weekend."

"No, Pete, I'm still bed-bound, and this is your busy season. It's more important that you rest so you can do your job. There will be plenty of time later when I'm in rehab and far better company."

"How did all this happen?"

Alex related how she had fallen coming down the ramp at Rabbit Island Airport. "Luckily, Dr. Norse, the famous neurologist, was on the plane. He saw what had happened and rescued me. I'm at Northwestern University Hospital in Chicago. And will be for at least another week, probably two."

"Then you need to return with me, and I will see that you get excellent care. I've already lined up a nurse and a physical therapist."

"Pete, not so fast. I appreciate this, but I want to go back to Rabbit Island. Miss Maggie has said I can stay with her until it's safe to return home."

"Alex, our weather is much better. Here you can have the sun. There, it is, what? Snow?"

"Possibly, but not likely this early. Rabbit Island's weather is not like the mainland. We do get snow, but usually not until late January."

"Think about it, you can always reconsider."

"Okay, Pete. But aren't you supposed to be working?"

"I had some free time and needed to talk with you to be sure you're okay."

"Thanks. I'm glad to talk with you. I can't tell you how much I appreciated having a nice place to stay in hiding. Have a good rest of the week and weekend."

Sunday morning, wishing she were home, Alex studied the skyline outside her hospital window. She suspected her room with a great view was thanks to Dr. Norse's efforts. The Chicago skyline was beautiful, but she would have traded it in a heartbeat for her part of Lake Michigan and Rabbit Island.

Her melancholy thoughts were interrupted by her phone. Answering it, she found Arvin Chesney, the editor of the Rabbit Island Updates, who asked her to tell her story to him. "I've heard Miss Maggie's, Captain Hamilton's, and Chief Pauls' version, but they only know their part."

"Arvin, there's not much more to tell. But if you have some questions that are not too detailed, I will try to answer them. First, as you no doubt know, I fell while getting off the plane. I guess I was too excited to be home and was rushing. I'm at Northwestern University Hospital and will probably be here for another two weeks. As soon as my doctor thinks it's okay, he will have me transferred to their rehab unit. Once he's satisfied with my progress and sure I can do my exercises myself, I hope to return to Rabbit Island and stay with Miss Maggie. End of story. Oh, and you can tell your readers I miss them all and will be home as soon as possible."

"Who is your doctor?"

"I'm lucky. I'm under the care of the famed neurologist Dr. Michael Norse, who will be on Rabbit Island this weekend with his wife. There's a story for you. Ask him how he knows the Duliamis."

"I think you've answered any questions I might have." He laughed, "You have to admit that since you arrived on Rabbit Island, things have been anything but calm."

"I know. But that's all over. From now on, I'm going to be very boring. Count on it."

"Dr. Lawson, I doubt if you'll ever be boring." He paused, "I send mine and many other Rabbit Island inhabitants' best wishes and hopes for a speedy recovery. I'll see you when you get home."

As Alex disconnected the call, she heard, "Ms. Lawson, time for your PT," a young female therapist said, entering her room. "I'm very pleased with your progress so far, but you have a long road ahead of you."

After the physical therapist had provided passive PT, Alex called the Rabbit Island Clinic. When Nora answered, she asked, "Nora, how are things going there? I wish I were with you."

"So do we. Without you, we are busier than usual. Thank heavens it's not summertime with more tourists. There's still enough with the fall color."

"How is it going with the electronic health records?"

"Great, Eleanor left us in good shape. We are easily connected to both Crescent City General and Downstate, meaning we only have to make a transfer note when we send them a patient. And Dr. Gould has really begun to appreciate them. Yesterday, he asked me, 'Why did it take us so long to join the modern world?' We are happy with the input screens that we created with Eleanor. They meet our needs. Eleanor said she would take our ideas back to Downstate with her. Even though we don't need her, I miss her. But I know she is just a phone call away."

"Is that Alex on the phone?" she heard Dr. Gould's voice ask. When Nora nodded yes, he said, "Let me talk to her." Taking the phone from Nora, he said, "Dr. Lawson, what do you mean abandoning us? We need you. I've been way too busy."

"Believe me, I didn't want to."

"You know, earlier, I was pretty stubborn. I didn't realize how much help you could be. Now I miss you. Hurry and get back to us, but not before you are healthy."

"Not to worry, I'll do as the doctor says. I don't want any long-term effects."

"I just hope you will be back here soon. The new housing development has been completed, and new residents are moving in, which brings us more full-time residents and kids. You take good care of yourself and return to work as soon as it's safe, but not before."

"I will, Dr. Gould."

After wishing her well, he handed the phone to Nora, who, as soon as he was out of earshot, said, "I can't wait for you to get back." She laughed, "He's been a bear and complaining that you should not have left us."

"Nora, it's nice to be missed, but I empathize with you. I miss the Clinic and will be glad to get back."

"But not until you are well. Once we get you back, we want you to stay well. I have to go. Another patient just came in. It was good to talk to you. Bye."

"Have a good weekend, Nora. Rest assured, I will be back ASAP! "

Alex lay back and marveled at how things had changed since April when she started working at the Clinic. She was pleased that Dr. Gould now accepted her and her role. She enjoyed working with him. He had a great deal to teach her, and she was a ready pupil, creating an excellent working relationship. Smiling with her thoughts, she relaxed and went to sleep.

20 Life in the Hospital

When Alex woke up the following day, she saw her father sitting in the chair by her bed. "Dad, what are you doing here?"

"Where do you expect me to be? My only daughter was kidnapped, rescued, then in hiding, and now in the hospital with a few broken vertebrae."

"Dad, I'm so glad to see you," Alex said as he got up, kissed her cheek, and stroked her hair. "I meant to call you, but didn't want to worry you. How did you find out where I am?"

"That Miss Maggie is a font of knowledge. It was she who called me, but not until you were released from the ICU and spent a few days in the regular hospital. I gave her heck for waiting so long, but she said you were not up to visitors. She knew I would take the first flight to Chicago as soon as I heard. She was right, and I will stay with you until you're released."

"After I'm out of here, I must go to rehab."

"Then you're coming home with me. We Gomes Islanders will see no more bad things happen to you."

Alex smiled. "Dad, this is the third offer I've had. First, Miss Maggie, then Pete, and now you. I'd be exhausted trying to go everywhere. I want to go home to Rabbit Island. You can come too if you want."

"So now you regard Rabbit Island as home."

"Yes, I do. That does not mean I've forgotten, or ever could, Gomes Island and you. But as you taught me after I lost

David, one has to move on."

"How about coming to your original home for Christmas? Nelson and your nieces will be there."

"If by then I'm able, I would love to. We always had such fun at Christmas."

"I promise, but only if I have medical permission to come."

"I never knew you to want medical, or for that matter, parental permission to do something."

"Maybe I've grown up. I know what Dr. Norse gave up for me, and I'll be forever grateful. If he gives me the okay, try and keep me away."

"Okay, that's the best I can expect. I want you to get well with no lingering side effects."

"Me too. I want to return to my work."

Her dad paused and studied her, "Have you renewed your relationship with Pete Herrison? Sorry, Harris. How is he?"

"He's great. He has a lovely home, er estate, loves his work, and helped to keep me safe. He let his home be invaded by me and a stranger. Do you watch his show?"

"Occasionally."

"Keep this a secret, but he had me do a bit for one of next season's shows. For all I know, it may be on the cutting room floor, but it was fun."

"So now, you're going to be an actress."

"No, Dad. I'm happy being a nurse practitioner."

"Are you again in a serious relationship with Pete?"

"No, just a brother-sister thing. It's fun to recall crazy things from our high school days, but it's just a good friendship. And he was a great host. If I had to be in hiding, it was nice to be with someone I knew, even though he was busy making next season's shows."

When lunch came, her dad took leave, "I'll be back this

evening. I'm going to O'Hare to see if I can see some of my old buddies. And look up George Frenworthy, the mechanic who saved my job, a 737, and plenty of passengers. I hear he's about to retire."

"Have a good time." After he left, Alex chuckled to herself. Her dad had to be doing something, and she was sure that sitting by her bedside was very dull for him. She suspected he might go home after a few days once he was sure his daughter was doing well. She was glad he had something to do because she spent much of the afternoon in PT.

Her dad returned just as she finished the early dinner that all hospitals serve. "How did your visit go?"

"Everyone was glad to see me. Several pilots that I worked with when they were first officers are now captains. The young lady who reminded me of you and is now a captain was in the pilot's lounge, and I was delighted to see her. When I flew with her, I knew she was captain material. I am glad the airline recognizes that women pilots can be just as good as men. Tammie Jo Shults of Southwest Airlines in 2019 certainly put that argument to rest when she saved the lives of almost 150 people after an engine exploded. The only fatality on that flight was a passenger who was almost sucked out of the plane but rescued by other passengers, only to die later."

"It's nice to see the progress women, and yes, men, have made in accepting us."

"Do you wish you had followed your original plan?"

"In some ways, I do. I love to fly, but am very happy as a nurse practitioner."

"Would you believe I was asked to return to work until I pointed out I was a fair way past the mandatory retirement age?"

"Do you miss flying an airliner?"

"It's a lot of responsibility. I'm not sure the public realizes the times we earn our salary, such as bad weather and when the unexpected happens. That's when you want a great pilot in the cockpit. The fact that the public doesn't know about most of these episodes is probably good, or they would quit flying."

"Seems the public is now addicted to flying, judging by the number of full flights."

"That's what keeps my pension solvent! After COVID, people had a pent-up wish to go somewhere, and they went and are still going. Flying has made the world much smaller, which is hard for some people to understand. Within twenty-four hours, one can be in almost any place on earth. Judging by the number of cargo planes, there is also a booming world economy."

"As you say, the genie is out of the bottle and short of a catastrophic war, it will stay out. Have you had dinner?"

"No, I was hoping to eat with you."

"Sorry, Dad, I'm enduring hospital fare. But the cafeteria has some good food. Where are you staying?"

"In the hotel for patients' relatives. They also have good food. You look tired. Maybe I'll go back to my room and let you get some rest."

"I have spent much of the day in PT, which is tiring."

Getting up to leave, he walked over to her bed, leaned down, kissed her, and said, "Good night. Sleep tight."

Laughing, she added, "And don't let the bed bugs bite, right? Good night to you, too."

Early the next morning, Dr. Norse entered her room, "Well, Colonel, the report on you is good. I can't see any reason why we can't send you to rehab this morning."

Opening her eyes, Alex said a little sleepily, "That is good news."

"The nurses report that you behaved and did not give them or anyone a hard time." He grinned, "And never once tried to get out of bed and help."

"I was tempted, but I didn't dare. These nurses are wonderful, and like most places, you are short-staffed."

"You know how it goes, the suits never think of those on the front lines when they are budgeting their salaries . . ."

"Only too well. By the way, how was your weekend on Rabbit Island?"

"Excellent. Even the weather cooperated. Your Miss Maggie insisted on having me and my wife to dinner."

"Ah yes, she has to be involved in everything. But we love her."

"I can see why. The best news of all is that Mrs. Duliami is almost completely well. And I'm discharging her to you. If she needs anything before you are working, Dr. Gould can take care of it. But I especially want you to follow up on her. I told her she can go back to work next week. Like you, forced idleness drives her nuts."

"I can empathize with that!"

"I'm going to arrange to have you transferred to our rehab unit after you have breakfast. You need to eat and keep your energy up to heal well. In another week, we'll do another CT scan to be sure all is well inside."

As with all hospital transfers, it took several hours before Alex was safely ensconced in the rehab unit. Her window view was not as nice as in the hospital, but at least it was not a wall. She could see a few trees and a park because the branches had lost most of their leaves. Before she was comfortably settled, she was whisked to PT for a workout. Then, a late lunch and that afternoon, another PT session.

After all that activity, Alex was tired and back in her new room. Before she was settled, her dad visited again.

"Had a time finding you. You were not in your regular room."

"No, Dad. I've progressed to rehab.

"I went to O'Hare again. George was off yesterday, but

today was happy to see me. He will retire at the end of the year. My wish is that he has taught the other mechanics what he knows, but that will be hard. I suspect so much of what he does and knows is by instinct, and he can't tell you what he knows. He taught me a lot. I swear, he can listen to an engine and tell you what's wrong."

"Glad you enjoyed seeing him."

"Also saw a few more of the pilots who were my first officers and are now captains. And met a few of the new crop of first officers. By the way, I've arranged for a tray for me tonight so we can enjoy dinner together."

"Dad, this is institutional food, remember?"

"The best part of the meal will be having you to eat it with."

"Alex, after they release you from rehab, can I convince you to change your mind and return to Gomes Island?"

"Dad, I've already told Miss Maggie I would go there. Much as I love you and Gomes Island, I need to start getting back in the mix on Rabbit Island."

"And go to work."

"I will not go to work until Dr. Norse says it is okay. Then I'll probably start part-time."

"I can understand. At least I will get to see you at Christmas. I know that Nelson and his girls will be happy about that."

"Dad, remember, only if Dr. Norse gives me permission. I would like to see them too."

"As long as you will try to visit."

"When do you expect to go back? I don't think sitting around here while I'm busy with PT and tired at night is any life for you. And you can't spend every day at O'Hare."

Her dad laughed. "Alex, you know me too well. Like you, I need to be busy. I'm still working with the Sea Scouts and the future pilots."

"I understand there is going to be a shortage of pilots. Any you train will be a credit to the profession."

"The shortage is here now. If I weren't over seventy, they would hire me yesterday."

"Do you wish you were back flying for Worldwide Airways?"

"In some ways, but it was good to see more of the former first officers I worked with now captains. As I told you yesterday, we old guys need to make room for the young. The new first officers I met appeared up to the job. And it's nice to know where I am every morning when I wake up."

"I can empathize with that! Why don't you go back tomorrow? You know firsthand that I am okay and getting better."

"If I can get the flights, I will. It used to be easy to fly free. Now, one has to fly stand-by."

"Get on the phone and see what you can do."

Her dad left the next day after she promised to call regularly.

During the week, Alex was kept busy with morning and afternoon PT.

Knowing that she had a day off from PT on Saturday morning, she could sleep in. She planned to have an easy day, perhaps walking around the unit and reading one of the rehab library books. In the middle of the afternoon, while she was sitting in a chair reading a book, she looked up and saw Pete.

"Pete, what a pleasant surprise."

"I told you I would visit you." He grinned, "Didn't you believe me?"

She laughed. "After all this time, I have learned to believe you. But this is still your busy season. Glad as I am to see you, aren't you burning the candle at both ends."

"Hey, Quinn Cass is unstoppable."

"Sometimes I think you think you are Quinn Cass and

immortal. Off the screen, no one writes the script."

Pete walked over to her, bent down, put his arms around her as much as he could with her neck collar on, and kissed her. "I know that. Rest assured, I'm returning early tomorrow and will study my lines on the flight. But I had to see for myself that you were doing well. I was pretty upset about your accident. Should have kept you an extra day, then you would have been stronger." He released her and pulled a chair up so he could sit close to her.

"Pete, did my scene make the final cut?"

"Certainly. And the director and producer are open to you doing more guest spots but with a larger role."

"Pete, you shouldn't be pulling strings for me. Did you forget that I have a job? One I like?"

"Alex, get this straight: my career and the show are very important to me. I would not be interested in having you do some guest spots if we did not think you would be good for the show."

Alex had her doubts about that. "This is not something we need to decide today."

"When will they let you out of here so you can come back to my home for more rehab?"

"Pete, you are very considerate, but I have just told my dad, and now I'm telling you, I'm going back to Rabbit Island and staying with Miss Maggie."

"Bummer."

After Alex ordered dinner for Pete, Pete entertained her with stories about the rise and fall of his career while Alex related some of her experiences in the military.

When they heard the trays in the hall, Pete reached into the bag he had brought with him and produced a bottle of wine and two glasses. "I have permission for you to have a glass of wine so we don't have to hide."

"Pete, you think of everything. This will hit the spot.

Perhaps help us forget this is institutional food."

He stood up to pour them each a glass of wine. "Are you glad I made this decision?"

Alex took the glass of wine he offered. "Yes, Pete. This was a good decision."

Surprisingly, dinner was not too bad and made better by the wine. As he was getting ready to leave, Pete left the bottle of wine and glasses on her table, saying. "I can't take these on the plane, so perhaps you can enjoy them while you are here."

"I'll think of you when I do."

The loudspeaker notified everyone that visiting hours were over. Before leaving, Pete helped Alex to stand and steadied her on her feet. "I hate to leave, but duty calls."

"Pete, you have made this a delightful afternoon and evening. Your visit has perked me up. The nurses are very nice but busy and don't have time to sit and talk." She laughed, "Not that I do either during the week. They keep me busy in the morning and afternoon, and I'm pretty tired by late afternoon. But seeing an old friend has been a real upper."

Pete carefully hugged Alex, avoiding her neck collar, and gave her a parting kiss. "Until we meet again. He released her, carefully helped her sit down, kissed her forehead, and left, waving to her. Alex smiled, thinking how lucky she was to have him as a friend.

Monday morning, Dr. Norse entered Alex's room. "If your report from your PT is good, tomorrow I'll let you return to Rabbit Island and Miss Maggie's care."

21 Alex Comes Home

A week later, Dr Norse visited Alex while she was eating breakfast. "Well, Colonel, your reports are good, and if the CT Scan I ordered is good, I don't know why you can't return to your Miss Maggie and Rabbit Island."

"When can I have the scan?"

"How about in 30 minutes?"

"Wow. I'll have time to get dressed. When will you let me know the result?"

He laughed, "Knowing your impatience, I'll read it immediately and get my good friend, Dr. Drummond, the radiologist, to back me up. Let's say, by noon today."

"Dr. Norse, much as I appreciate everything you and the staff have done for me, I am anxious to return to Rabbit Island."

"To Rabbit Island, but only if you stay with Miss Maggie. You should not live alone until probably January."

"Will I be well enough to visit my father for Christmas in late December?"

"Where does he live?"

"Near Portland, Maine."

"I think you should be okay, but I expect a good report from Dr. Gould before you go."

"Understood."

"I'll see you this noon with the report."

When he left, Alex finished the last of her breakfast, took her last drink of coffee, and put on her clothes, the same ones she had worn for what seemed forever. "It will be good to get home and have different clothes—I'm sick of these," she said aloud.

Once back in her room after her scan, Alex did more PT and waited impatiently for noon and Dr. Norse's visit.

About fifteen minutes before noon, he appeared in her doorway, smiling. "Well, Colonel, your scan looks great. When do you want to be discharged?"

"Early tomorrow. I can have one of the Rabbit Island Air planes come and get me."

Laughing, he told her, "The helicopter, of course. I see you want to leave the same way you came."

"Why not?" She smiled. "Thanks for the quick report." As Dr. Norse left, Alex called Miss Maggie and told her she could come home the next day. Almost before Alex had the news out, Miss Maggie was telling her of all the plans that were in place for her stay with her. "Does Pete know you are coming back to Rabbit Island?"

"I have tried to tell him, but I'm not sure he has processed it. Both my dad and Pete wanted me to finish rehabbing with them, but I wanted to be back on Rabbit Island. I suspect Pete will visit again as soon as they have next fall season's episodes in the can."

"Visit again?"

"Yes, he was here last Saturday afternoon. It was good to see him. And he left me a bottle of wine and wine glasses. I enjoyed the rest of the bottle yesterday."

Hoping Alex would get back together with Tony, Miss Maggie was not happy to hear that. "What is your status with Pete?"

"Good friends."

"Nothing more?" Miss Maggie asked hopefully.

Instead of answering, Alex changed the subject. "I ordered the food staples that I might need for the winter, when the *Queen* might or might not operate. Will you help me put them away when they come? I had them sent to my house. They should be there early next week."

"You should have had them sent here. But perhaps I can take you to your house, and you can supervise me putting them away."

Alex smiled. She knew Miss Maggie meant that Alex should learn where she put them. "I would appreciate that."

"Oh, I almost forgot to tell you. Bert Nelson, Tony, and Chief Pauls took your boat out of the water, and it's all covered up and winterized."

"I owe them. That was so nice of them. I planned to do it just before Thanksgiving."

"You'll be here for Thanksgiving. We'll have a celebration dinner."

"I forgot it's almost that time."

"Once we get you home, you will get reoriented. By the way, Tony wants to come and get you." She paused and added emphatically. "Alone."

"Oh?"

"And I want you to listen to him. What you ultimately decide is up to you, but you owe him a hearing."

"If he insists," she said grudgingly, thinking she did not need to hear how Gina was so much better suited to him and his lifestyle. "But you should come with him."

"Not this time."

After Miss Maggie told her that Tony would be coming alone to bring her back to Rabbit Island and that she should listen to him, Alex wished she could take a commercial flight home rather than have Tony formally explain why he broke up with her. She knew better than to protest. She needed Miss Maggie's support because she would probably have to stay with her for the next several months. And she wanted to be on Rabbit Island, even without Tony.

At her last PT session that afternoon, she thanked the two PT personnel who had supervised her rehab. She still had to wear a neck collar, just as she had since her surgery. It was not the most comfortable thing in the world, but she had become used to it and knew it would not be forever. She was tired after she finished putting her things in the duffle bag Miss Maggie had previously sent. Lying down on her bed, she looked out her window, hoping that maybe a few trees would still have their leaves when she returned to Rabbit Island.

"Good evening, Beautiful."

Looking up, she saw Tony standing in the doorway. "Hello, yourself. Aren't you a little early? I won't be released until tomorrow."

Tony entered her room, "Alex, may I talk to you?"

She stared out the window and said unenthusiastically. "If you want."

"Remember the afternoon when I left you at Crescent City General?"

She moved further away from Tony and continued to stare out the window. "How could I forget?"

Tony stood stiffly. "Alex," he stopped and hesitantly looked at her. "Gina told me that a nurse told her to tell us you would be delayed, and we should return to Rabbit Island. She added that you said I should take her sailing because she knew I was counting on an afternoon of sailing."

"That's a big lie."

Tony sighed and looked towards the window, "I'm only telling you what Gina told me. I know now that you did not say those things. And that Gina lied."

She looked hard at Tony. "But you didn't think to check with me?"

He hung his head. "My mistake, one of the biggest I've ever made." He raised his head and looked at Alex. "I am deeply sorry and wish I could change that. When we got back, you were so irritated, I knew you were incapable of listening to reason. I fully intended to try again later. But then you had already replaced me with that Pete Harris."

Alex lay there, mulling over what he told her. Had she really been so stupid and perhaps angry at the thought that she had lost Tony? Finally, she looked at him. "I hate to admit it, but you're right. I would not have listened. I never wanted to break up, but perhaps you can understand my feelings about what happened. I would probably have been more rational if I had not felt so hurt. Emotions can easily trip you up."

"The next day, I was not sure you were ready to be rational, so I let Gina convince me to take her to Steve's Island Resort for Sunday brunch. And you were there. With that TV star Pete Harris' arm around you, I figured I could not compete with him and let Gina lead me on, hoping to make you jealous."

"You succeeded. And I was hoping to make you jealous."

"You did. And then I had to carry on with Gina. She's not all bad, a great pilot, but prone to the little green monster and too much prejudice."

"And has a drop-dead figure to boot. She hated me from the moment you started helping me get my private pilot's license back."

"As I said, the little green monster." He paused, "Alex, I fired her after that episode where she refused to fly you here. I would have fired her for that alone, but her bigoted comments about Dr. Norse did not represent what Rabbit Island Air is all about, and I will not tolerate employees who say things like that or even think that way."

"Tony, doesn't that leave you short a pilot?"

"Brad Teaberry has been helping out, and I have a lead on a replacement. A man this time, no more jealousy. Now, the big question. Are you still involved with Pete Harris?"

She was quiet momentarily, then looked at Tony, "Do you want me to be?"

"No!"

"Then I'm not. It's just a brother-sister relationship. We had a past, but it is a past. Besides, he's still in love with Brittany. She was right that night when she sang, 'You ain't woman enough to steal my man' to me. I'm not."

"Do you want to be?"

"No, Tony, I don't."

"Can we start again?"

"I would like nothing better."

With a broad smile, he told her, "You don't know how happy that makes me. I have missed you, our evenings talking over the day, and everything we used to do together."

Studying Tony, Alex said, "I, too, have missed them, and especially you."

"That didn't stop you from going with that Pete Harris."

"Why should it have? You were obviously with Gina, and I learned that one must move on. As you know, since I lost my husband, you were not my first loss."

"I hope I won't ever again be a loss."

Alex smiled but felt tears in her eyes as she looked at Tony, who seemed very contrite. "I would like to make the past few months a temporary blip in our relationship."

Tony's expression changed to a broad smile. "Alex, you don't know how happy this makes me." Careful of her neck brace, Tony hugged her as much as possible. "Dr. Norse said I could take you out to dinner tonight, and he gave me the name of a nice restaurant near here."

Surprised but happy that Tony had come a day early and wanted to take her to dinner, Alex said, "I'm delighted to have dinner with you. And real food instead of institutional fare will make this a double treat."

"Tomorrow, after your official release, I will take you home in the Cessna. I found a little airport near here, and we can take an Uber there. The helicopter is scheduled for a job tomorrow, or I would have brought that. And the 8-seater is larger than we need. When you are better, we'll return to your multi-engine certification." He smiled at her, "I might even let you fly a little tomorrow. Keep up your skills. That is if you feel able."

"One step at a time." She pointed at her neck collar, "With this thing, I'm not that flexible. For the next few months, I will leave the flying to you. But next year . . .," she smiled.

Dinner out with Tony at the small restaurant Dr. Norse had recommended was a special time for Alex. Making the dinner even better, she felt it was the beginning of a new relationship with him, one she thought was on a better footing, one in which they both could release their old baggage and trust more.

The following day, near noon, Dr. Norse released Alex. Taking off in the Cessna, Alex felt again the joy of flight. She was excited about returning to Rabbit Island and wanted to tell Tony to go faster, but instead, she decided to enjoy this time with him. She smiled, happy that their relationship was back on an even keel. No one can know the future, but Alex felt secure in the relationship this time.

Before landing, as they circled the Rabbit Island Airport, Alex saw a crowd on the tarmac in front of the Rabbit Island Air hangars, waving at them and holding a sign reading, "Welcome home. Don't leave us again."

"Tony, how can they get out on the tarmac?"

"With the big boss gone, who will stop them?" He gave her a big grin, "Did you ever try to stop Miss Maggie? Anyway, this is not the commercial terminal."

She turned to Tony, "Did you know about this?"

He briefly glanced at her and left the question unanswered, but was smiling as he performed the tasks necessary for a smooth landing. As the plane taxied to a stop in front of the hangar, Brad Teaberry rushed over to open the door for her. Much as she would have liked to leap out and greet everyone, with her neck brace, it wasn't easy to extricate herself from the Cessna. With Brad's help, she finally put her feet on Rabbit Island soil.

Many 'Happy Returns' and 'So glad to see yous' were exchanged, and gentle hugs were given before Alex could move towards the terminal building.

"Okay, folks, we've shown Dr. Larson that we're glad she's back, but she could be tired," Chief Pauls told the group. "She's here for good."

"Absolutely," Alex said, laughing, "You couldn't get rid of me if you tried."

In the crowd, Alex saw Arvin Chesney making notes and directing a photographer to get pictures of her arrival. As she approached the terminal, he approached her and said, "How about a few words for the Press."

Alex laughed and said, "You can tell everyone I am delighted to be back and won't go roaming again."

"Thanks for your time, Alex."

"As soon as I get the plane put away, I'll join you at Miss Maggie's," Tony said.

It was a tired Alex that finally reached Miss Maggie's. Minnie looked at her and saw that she looked exhausted. "Dr. Larson, how about a little rest and then a snack? Your room is ready."

"Thanks, Minnie. I didn't realize how tired the flight and all this would make me."

"We're going to take extra good care of you until you are ready to move back to your home."

She smiled at Minnie. "I'm sure you will,"

Following Minnie's advice, Alex rested for about thirty minutes, then came downstairs. As she was enjoying Minnie's snack, Tony joined them. After eating, Miss Maggie said, "Okay, Alex, time to do some exercises. Tony, you go back to work. We will expect you for dinner."

"Yes, Miss Maggie," Tony said with a smile.

Alex groaned. "Exercises? No time for more rest?"

Miss Maggie gave Alex a stern look. "Today, you have not done one single exercise. All you've done is fly home with Tony." Miss Maggie brought out a list of exercises with illustrations that Dr. Norse, at her request, had had the physical therapists at the Northwestern Rehab Center send her. She took Alex to one of the bedrooms upstairs, which was outfitted with any equipment Alex might need for her exercises.

"Miss Maggie, you overdid yourself."

"There is no way I'm going to let you vegetate."

Alex followed the routine she had established at the rehab center. After an hour, she relaxed and then a little later did more exercises. Before she knew it, it was time for dinner.

"Congratulations. I checked on you now and then, and you were working hard."

Alex laughed. "I had a choice?"

Miss Maggie smiled. "No. According to Dr. Norse, the answer to the second question of when I can get back to work is, 'It's up to you.' He trusts your judgment. I suggest you wait until after Thanksgiving, which is next week." She paused and looked at Alex, "Dr. Gould would have you back today if I let him."

"A big change from last April."

"Further, I understand that he and Nora have taken to the electronic records very well."

"I'll have to relearn what Nora taught me about using the EHR before all this happened. Be a good way to get my feet wet again at work."

"We'll see."

Tony joined them for dinner, but Miss Maggie told him, "Alex needs her rest, and you need to go home for the night. Can you make it a habit to have dinner with us every evening? I think Alex wants that." What she did not say was 'so do I.' Her hope for keeping them on the island would be helped if they stayed together.

22 Thanksgiving

That evening, after Tony left Alex at Miss Maggie's, where she is staying until she can live alone, Pete called Alex, wanting to know how she was. "I wish you had come out here to recover. You can still change your mind, you know. We're having wonderful weather."

"Pete, I know. But you have your life to live. Tony, the gentleman I was with before we met on that fateful morning, and I are back together. And I think you're still in love with Brittany."

"She won't have anything to do with me."

"I think you could be wrong. Earlier that evening at the party at her house, when you were acting very romantically with me, I could see her looking at you enviously. And before that, I saw you looking at her the same way. I don't know what caused the breakup, but I think she might be receptive."

"As soon as she knows you and that man are together, she will think I want to date her again because you threw me over."

"You don't know that for sure. I hope you'll think about it. What do you have to lose?"

"Forget it. I called to tell you that sometime this spring, you can watch yourself on TV. I'll let you know the exact date when I learn it."

Alex laughed, "You mean you prevailed on the director to include it, and he weakened. I figured I was out when he didn't want a second take."

"Alex, we've already had this conversation. I did not influence any decisions. And both of us still want you back next year for a few segments. You will be a recurring character as a nurse practitioner."

"Pete, I'm not an actress."

"Think of the publicity for Rabbit Island and nurse practitioners."

"We'll see," was all Alex would say.

During the next few weeks at Miss Maggie's, a routine was developed: Alex would exercise in the morning, then a light lunch, a nap, and more exercises in the afternoon, and then Tony would join them for dinner.

Before they knew it, it was Thanksgiving morning. Looking out the window from her bed at Miss Maggie's, Alex could see it would be a nice day. Besides overseeing Alex's activities, Miss Maggie and Minnie had spent the last week planning the Thanksgiving Dinner. It was to be a welcome home affair, and in addition to Tony, Miss Maggie had invited Ann and Captain Chuck Hooper, Camille and Chief Pauls (Irv), Brad Teaberry, and Bert Nelson from the marina, as well as Dr. Gould and his wife, Charlotte. Alex was looking forward to seeing everyone in a social situation.

After finishing her exercises, she showered and dressed carefully. Not wanting to change her clothes, she came down to breakfast dressed for dinner. The smell of turkey permeated the air as she entered the kitchen. "Minnie, I'll just get a little cereal for breakfast. Don't stop what you are doing. I want to keep a big appetite for dinner!"

Eyeing Alex, Miss Maggie inquired, "Young lady, have you done your morning exercises?"

"Of course! I wouldn't dream of skipping them, even for Thanksgiving," Alex answered mockingly and politely. Then she turned to Miss Maggie and said, "And Happy Thanksgiving to you," adding, "Also to you, Minnie." Getting her cereal, she asked, "Is there anything I can do to help?"

"Just get your cereal and go take it easy." Miss Maggie ordered. "And stay out of the dining room."

"Yes, ma'am," Alex responded, smiling as she entered the great room. Eating her cereal, she thought about her call from Pete. His promise to visit again in the spring unnerved her. She was glad to be back with Tony and did not want to encourage him.

"I wonder if I could talk to Brittany," she said aloud, then added, "It's probably not a good idea, and she probably wouldn't accept my call anyway. Still, I want to try. What have I got to lose?" Finally, she decided to do it and figured that today was as good a day as any despite it being Thanksgiving. She won't be working.

At noon Rabbit Island time, she placed the call. "Good morning, Alex," Britany answered cheerily. "So glad you called. I will be on Rabbit Island next spring to do a week's shows at Steve's Island Resort. I'd love to see you again."

"That's wonderful. I will look forward to it. Will Pete come with you?"

There was silence on the line, "Why? Do you want to renew your relationship with him?"

"Brittany, I'm in love with a gentleman here on Rabbit Island. But my observation at your party was that Pete still loves you. Also, I may be completely wrong, but my observations made me think you may still have a soft spot in your heart for him. I have no idea what caused your breakup, but I'm pretty sure he's regretting it."

"You mean after you dumped him."

"Brittany, I did not dump him. There never was anything there except old high school remembrances. We are like brother and sister and not romantically involved. I think he used me to try to make you jealous, just as I did him to make my friend here jealous. My strategy almost resulted in love lost. I want to hope it did not do that for you." There was silence on the other end of the line.

Finally, Brittany responded thoughtfully, "I'll think about what you have said, but no promises."

"If you decide this is a good time, you may need to contact him. He doesn't think you will talk to him, so he doesn't feel free to call you."

"Stubborn Pete, yes?"

"And pride."

"I have my pride, too."

"I know, but I suspect you are a little more adult about it than most men can be."

Brittany laughed. "You may be on to something."

"Anyway, no matter what you decide, I hope you have a nice Thanksgiving."

"No plans for dinner, but I'm going down to the shelter and help serve the Thanksgiving Dinner. They need the help."

"Very generous of you. I admire you for doing that."

"Then I'll probably join a few of the volunteers for leftover dinner."

"After all that, you'll be tired."

"You bet, and then I can sleep well. Anyway, Alex, thanks for calling. I will think about what you said, but remember, no promises."

"I understand. Meanwhile, have a good day."

Later that afternoon, as the guests arrived for Thanksgiving Dinner, Alex was able to greet each one. Welcoming Ann Hooper, she asked, "Are you set to do your practicum in our office?"

"If you and Dr. Gould still want me."

"Of course we do," Dr. Gould answered. "Dr. Larson, here, has shown me how much help nurse practitioners can be to a practice."

"What date can you start?" Alex asked.

"I was thinking the first week in February."

Once comfortably seated with glasses of wine, Alex told the group, "I need to thank you, Irv, Bert, Brad, and Tony, for making La Senora ready for the winter."

"We were glad to do it. It was the least we could do for you while you were in rehab," Bert said.

"Ditto for me," chimed in both Irv and Tony.

"Dinner is served," Minnie announced to the group. Walking into the dining room, Alex was smiling,but that soon became laughter. A big sign on the wall read, "Don't Go Wandering Again."

"I didn't choose to this time," Alex said amid laughter and boos. "Now, let's eat. I know how hard Miss Maggie and Minnie worked on this dinner.

As Alex was getting ready for bed that evening, she wondered about the wisdom of her call to Brittany. Well, it's done. I wonder if I would have done it if I had thought about it longer. I was impulsive.

Two nights later, Pete called to tell her that Brittany had called him and asked him to drop by for a drink when he had time. "Did a little bird talk to her? Like you?"

"What makes you think that? Is it possible she may have realized that you are attracted to each other and acted on it."

"Are you going to do as she asked?"

"Tonight. I'll let you know how it goes."

"I wish you luck!"

Monday, Dr. Norse called Alex to ask how she was.

"I'm doing well. I have more energy, and I'm doing the exercises religiously. How long do I have to wear this cervical collar?"

"I'd like you to have cervical x-rays and be evaluated by a neurologist before I answer. If you have been faithful in doing your exercises, we may be able to let you stop wearing it. I understand the neurologist at Downstate comes to Crescent City General once a month. I will contact him and have him order X-rays and set you up for an appointment the next time he is there."

"Wonderful! And, can I go home to Maine for Christmas if I'm okay?"

"I would think so."

After hanging up, Alex was elated. She hoped these things could be scheduled quickly. Meanwhile, she entertained the idea of going to the Clinic that afternoon. When she broached the idea to Miss Maggie, after she told her about her conversation with Dr Norse, she agreed and said she would take her.

Dropping Alex off at the Rabbit Island Clinic, Miss Maggie told her, "Call me when you want to come home."

"I will."

"And don't get overtired."

Alex was tempted to say, "Yes, Mother," but instead, Alex answered, "I won't."

Nora greeted her as she entered the reception room. "Are we glad to see you! But no patient visits yet. Miss Maggie has given strict orders."

Alex laughed. "That Miss Maggie! Not today, but I hope next week to be able to do patient visits."

"If you had time, you could help me refresh using the EHR."

"That can be arranged," Nora told her as Dr. Gould entered the reception room.

"Dr. Larson, do we have you back?"

"Not so fast, Doctor," Nora interjected. "She's under strict orders only to work a little on the EHR."

"When do we get you back, even part-time?"

Alex related her morning phone conversation with Dr. Norse and ended by saying, "I hope next week. But I need some time at Christmas. I promised my dad I would visit him over the holidays."

"If you will cover New Year's, I think we can work that out."

The afternoon passed quickly. When Miss Maggie drove Alex back to her house, she said, "The groceries you ordered for the winter are at your house. I know Tony has been checking on things, and he told me. And you have appointments tomorrow at City General for your X-ray and evaluation by the neurologist. Tony said he would take you over and bring you back. This time of year, there is only a once-a-day round trip by the *Queen*."

"Wow, that was fast! I only just talked to Dr. Norse."

The reports from her X-ray and the neurologist were good, and Alex was able to remove her cervical collar. "It feels a little weird," Alex said as she took it off for the last time. Her exercise routine was also reduced to a few exercises once a day.

That evening, Tony said. "I see your nonperishables are at your house. "Saturday, we can get them stowed away."

"I was going to help her." Miss Maggie said.

"Let me do it, then I too will know where they are," Tony responded.

Miss Maggie smiled. Knowing this was a sign that he and Alex were back together again, she uncharacteristically agreed.

After they put away Alex's winter grocery stock on Saturday, Tony, having planned this with Miss Maggie, took Alex to the Busted Jib for dinner. Knowing she was coming, a big crowd was waiting, and she had a chance to talk with everyone. She returned to Miss Maggie's tired but happy.

On Sunday afternoon, Alex received a call from Pete. "I followed your advice and had that drink with Brittany."

"How did it go?"

"Let me answer by saying I will come with her this spring when she does her week at Steve's Resort."

"Tony and I will welcome you both."

"I still think you played Cupid. Are you and that man still together?"

"Yes, and I think we will stay that way.:

"Are you happy about it?"

"Yes, Pete. Very."

"I'm glad. I think we helped each other out when needed. Remember, I will always be available to help you."

"Pete. And I you. I'm so glad we revived our friendship, but now in a more grown-up way. I don't regret a moment I spent with you, either when we were young or recently."

"I feel the same way."

23 The Holidays

After disconnecting Pete's call, Alex smiled. The way things worked out with Pete, Brittany, and her and Tony was perfect for her way of thinking. The future looked bright.

The week after Thanksgiving, Alex worked half days at the Clinic. That week, she found time to prepare for mentoring Ann Hooper. She had already received guides from the University and wanted to review them. She told Nora, "Ann will start her preceptorship the first week of February. After Ann finishes her preceptorship and does her capstone project, she will be our second nurse practitioner."

After hearing that, Nora laughingly told Alex. "Because she's here, don't you go running off again."

"Not to worry. I'm sure I'll still be needed. With all the new residents, there will be enough work for all of us. I'm looking forward to having her here."

"Dr. Gould confided to me that now that he knows that nurse practitioners are beneficial at the Clinic, he will be cutting back more," Nora told her. "I think his wife is happy about this."

"There is something that I need to do—see how the Novik family is doing after the truth about Marta's molestation came out. I'm going to call June Westen at Crescent City General."

Surprisingly, June answered on the first ring. "Hi, Alex. I heard you have had interesting experiences, going into hiding, falling on the tarmac, and injuring yourself."

"All that is history now. I called you to find out what happened to Marta."

"That chapter is not over. I think I told you she was pregnant."

"Yes."

"She denied the pregnancy. Asked how it could be. Woefully ignorant of too many facts of life. When she miscarried at six weeks, all she would say was, "I would never carry that creature's baby. He's a terrible person. The world does not need another person like him.""

"Wow. How did Marta's family react?"

"Presented with the facts, including the DNA tests that we did that first morning and the DNA tests on the products of conception showing Cedric to be the father, the mother relented. But her father still insisted she led him on."

"Even when he learned about the suit against Cedric by the woman who accused him of being her baby's father?"

"He just told Marta, 'But that girl is not you.'"

"Is Cedric still running loose?"

"No, they were able to convict him of statutory rape. The court determined he was a person of authority to Marta, and she could not resist. With the evidence, I hope the father can eventually work through his guilt. It has to be hard to realize that he was the one who brought this on her. Not unusual to try and blame Marta."

"Where is Marta now?"

"She's living with an aunt in Alpena, Michigan. And, freed of the burden of what was happening, plus weekly counseling, she is beginning to live up to her potential. She is now playing on a girls' after-school softball team. Helping her to feel better about herself is her acknowledgment that she prevented her younger sister from having to go through this."

"Miss Maggie tells me the family still lives on Rabbit

Island."

"I've talked with Camille and Chief Pauls and learned that they were able to keep this off the gossip mill. Camille tells me that the younger sister is doing okay at school. Not well, just okay."

"Any hint of a prognosis?"

"Can't tell, but the family's counselor told me the father is beginning to accept what happened and wants to make it up to Marta. But Marta, although she wants to see her sister and mother, does not want to see her father."

"So, there is room on that end for improvement if there will ever again be a resemblance of a family."

"Alex, sometimes my work gets me down. These situations hurt. Rape is a way for insecure men to keep women in what they consider 'their place.' It leaves a stain that only time, counseling, and a determined person can learn to live with."

"I understand. I thank you for your help with this family."

"And let's hope the help bears fruit."

"I still owe you a cup of coffee. If they ever let me off on my own, I will get over to the mainland and buy you one."

"You don't owe me anything. All in my line of work. Something I need to get back to. A victim of a gunshot is being admitted, and I'm needed. Get well."

"I will. And keep the coffee pot hot."

With permission from Dr. Norse and with Tony's help, the first weekend in December Alex moved back to her home. The understanding was that Tony would also live there. Sunday evening, as they enjoyed their first dinner in her home after moving back, Alex said, "Tony, I'm going to be spending Christmas with my family on Gomes Island. My brother, Nelson, and his family will be there too. Can you come with me?"

Tony hesitated, "I don't want to horn in on a family reunion."

"Tony, if I read things correctly, you are now family."

"Alex, I guess I never thought of our relationship like this, but if you are okay with it, so am I."

"Then, how about coming with me? I know we will have to buy tickets. There are never standby seats available at this time of year. Or do you have plans to visit your family?"

"Alex, the only family I have is my sons."

"When was the last time you saw them?"

" While you were in hiding in California, I was able to go see them for a weekend. They will visit me for a few days, starting on the Sunday after Christmas until New Year's Eve. I want them to meet you. And you to meet them."

"While they are here, you must stay with them in your apartment. And spend your free time with them."

"I will miss you."

"Tony, we have most of the year. You only have a few days. Tell you what, I will have you all over for dinner Wednesday night if that is ok. I don't mean to pry, but don't you have any other family?"

"A sister, but she was one of the few nurses in Vietnam, and she was killed there. My parents were killed in an automobile accident shortly thereafter."

"Tony, I'm so sorry. I didn't know."

"I didn't want to tell you earlier."

"I should have asked. Especially that day when we brought La Barca to her new home on Rabbit Island. I'm afraid I was too self-centered."

"I probably wouldn't have told you then anyway. I guess the friendliness and family-like atmosphere of Rabbit Island was one of the reasons I bought Rabbit Island Air and moved here before I retired. It doesn't substitute 100% for a family, but it's the closest thing to it." He paused, then looked seriously at Alex, "That is, until you." Tony looked at the floor. "I was devastated when we broke up." Looking up, he said, "Forgive my blindness. I let Gina lead me astray."

"Tony, maybe we needed a break to reevaluate our feelings."

"But you had Pete."

"And you had Gina."

"And we both teamed up with others to make each other jealous. It worked! Are you sure you are not still in love with Pete?"

"Tony, trust me, I'm not. In high school, we were inseparable, but this is now. We live in different worlds. Our relationship is like brother and sister." Alex paused, then told him the news about Pete and Brittany. "When they are here in the spring, the four of us can do something together."

"That should be interesting."

"Back to my original question, will you join me for Christmas on Gomes Island? We will be back on the Sunday after Christmas. You could have your boys meet us at O'Hare, then fly with us back to Rabbit Island."

"First things first. I'll have to see if I can get away, and if so, for how long. I'm assuming Dr. Gould has okayed this for you. What days do you plan to be away?"

"Christmas this year is on a Thursday. I was thinking of leaving sometime Christmas Eve and returning the following Sunday."

"I think I can make it. Bill Yazzie will be here. Alaska is too far to go. Let's hope Brad Teaberry is also available. And our new pilot is almost through with reinstating his multiengine license. There are already a few charters on the books, but they should be able to manage those."

"Do your boys have reservations to visit you?"

"Yes, and they are scheduled on the last Blue Water Air flight to Rabbit Island the Sunday after Christmas and back on New Year's Eve."

"That will work for us. How about later this afternoon we get our airplane reservations?"

Ten days later, Alex and Tony were welcomed at the Portland, Maine airport by Alex's dad. "Hon, so glad you could come," her dad said as he embraced her. Then he turned to Tony and said in an equally welcoming voice, "Captain Hamilton, we are all delighted that you could Did it make you want to jockey those big boys through the clouds again?"

"Captain Middleton, you forget I'm still flying. Not the big birds as you call them, but little ones and one, as you said, "Whose wings are not a permanent fixture. How about you? Do you miss the big birds?"

"Sometimes. But I am glad to be retired and able to plan my life. If you are going to stay with us, you'll have to call me Gus."

"And please call me Tony."

"Gather your things, and we'll head for the dock and our boat to Gomes Island. Gomes is much smaller than Rabbit Island. We don't even have an airfield."

"If what Alex has told me is true, it's even too small for a school."

Shortly after boarding their boat, they reached the Middleton dock on Gomes Island. Alex's brother, Nelson, sister-in-law, Nina, and two nieces, Samantha, now twelve, and seven-year-old Abigail, welcomed them. As they stepped onto the dock, Nelson hugged his sister, then turned to Tony, "Welcome to our motley family. We are delighted to have you join us for the holidays."

"By the way, Alex, your friend, Mia Trumble, is home. I'm sorry to have to tell you, but her mom is not doing well."

"I'm so sorry. I remember how she had hot chocolate and cookies ready after we would return from sledding on our little hill."

"Both Mia and her mom are looking forward to seeing you."

Christmas morning followed the Middleton custom that anyone under 18 could open their stocking before breakfast, but had to wait to open their other presents. Samantha and Abigail were used to this and, surprisingly, waited until seven o'clock to get everyone up. Alex smiled, glad for the extra sleep.

The only thing missing was snow! The weather report had promised it, but it was a false promise. The temperature, however, was in the twenties. Samantha and Abigail were disappointed they could not go sledding like last year. Still, Christmas Day, the sky was blue, and the family bundled up and followed a well-worn trail around half of the island.

"This is not as much fun as sledding, but I guess we have to make do," Samantha said as the youngsters enjoyed hot chocolate and the adults a hot toddy after an hour's walk.

"Daddy, can't we stay until it snows?" Abigail asked.

"Sorry, Abigail, we have to go back tomorrow. We've already been here a week, and Samantha has a play rehearsal on Saturday."

"Boo," Abigail responded, "Why does Samantha have to be in a silly old play?"

Everyone ignored her, and she soon walked off to enjoy her new typewriter. Like her father, she was intrigued by writing and spent the rest of the afternoon writing a story about the squirrels they saw on their walk.

Friday morning, there was a rush to get the Nelson Middleton family to the airport. The girls were subdued on the boat trip across to the Portland dock, where their boat docked when they were in town. "Next year, can't we stay longer?" Abigail asked as the boat docked.

"That's a long time away, but you can come again in the summer," her mother, Nina, told her. "

24 Gomes Island

As Alex, Tony, and her dad were having lunch after taking Alex's brother, Nelson, and his family to the airport, Alex's dad asked, "Who would like to go flying this afternoon?"

"I'm going to see Mia Trumble and her mom this afternoon. You guys go and have a good time," Alex replied.

"See you for supper."

"Translation, you want open-faced turkey sandwiches made by me," Alex laughingly said.

"Is there any other kind?"

"Go! Get out of here while I read my new book before I visit the Trumbles."

Just as Alex closed her book to get ready to go down the road to see her friend, her phone rang. "Alex, get Mia's father and have him take you to Rocky Cove. Two people are floating in the water near there. We also see what looks like the wreckage of a boat. They must have hit the rocks. They have life jackets on, but in this 45-degree water, they will not last long. We'll circle them until you get there."

"I'm on my way."

As soon as she told Mr. Trumble the information, the two were quickly out the door, down to the Trumble's dock, lowering the boat, and casting off. "Look for Dad's plane," Alex said. "He will be circling them."

Rounding the corner of the island, they could see the two survivors. Mr. Trumble wasted no time getting to them and instructing Alex to put down his boarding ladder. Between the two of them, they were able to get both survivors aboard, although it was difficult, as they were both weak.

As soon as they were safely aboard, Alex motioned to her dad that all was well. Then, she hurriedly led the survivors to the little cabin. Although not heated, it was at least out of the wind, which was beginning to become stronger.

Mr. Trumble proceeded to his dock as fast as it was safe while Alex insisted that the two survivors get out of their wet clothes. Then she rummaged through the closet near the bow of the boat and found some towels and blankets.

"If I take these off, I'll freeze," the young woman said.

"You'll freeze if you don't take them off. You can't even begin to warm up with wet clothes on. Dry yourself with these towels and wrap a blanket around you. We'll soon be at the dock, and then we can get you into a warm house."

Leaving the survivors to get out of their wet clothes, Alex told Mr. Trumble, "Call Mia and have her meet us at the dock with warm blankets. These two are close to hypothermia."

Returning to the boat cabin, she said, "I'm Dr. Alex Lawson, a nurse practitioner. Your captain is Mr. Trumble. Who are you?"

"I'm Noah Wilson, and this is my wife, Rose Wilson. We're on our honeymoon. We have a reservation at the Landis Resort on Ares Island. That is where we were going when we hit a rock and broke up."

"Why didn't you take the ferry?"

"We wanted to have a boat there. I understand there are no boats for rent on that island. I've been driving boats since I was seven. I grew up on a lake in the Ozarks."

"I'm afraid Casco Bay is a little different from what you

are used to," Alex said wryly.

"We were doing fine until we hit something under the water."

"This area is called Rocky Cove, and at high tide, which it is now, there are many underwater rocks that can rip a boat to pieces," Alex informed him.

"Guess that was what we hit. They should be marked with something," Noah said.

They could see Mia with the warm blankets as they approached the dock. She helped the two survivors get on the dock, then led the way to the house. Alex stayed behind to help Mr. Trumble tie up the boat and get it out of the water.

Approaching the house, Alex heard Mia call, "Alex, get in here. The young lady is shivering up a storm. What should I do?"

"Draw a tub of warm water, not hot, and put her in it. Then get them both some hot chocolate."

After getting Rose out of her underwear and testing the water, Alex helped her into the tub, then waited with her for the hot chocolate that Mia soon brought. Meanwhile, Mr. Trumble helped Noah shed the rest of his clothes and put him in warm clothing. Taking a sip of the hot chocolate, Noah said, "Thank you, Mr. Trumble, we were nearly goners."

About the time the survivors were dressed in warm clothes and relaxed, Tony and Gus returned to the island. Finding the house empty and suspecting Alex might be at the Trumbles, they lost no time getting there.

As they walked into the Trumbles, Gus said, "The weather is turning bad. I think the snow we did not get before Christmas may be on the way . . ." Seeing the survivors, he asked, "What were you guys doing out in a boat in Casco Bay this time of year?"

"We were going to Ares Island and the Landis Resort."

"Where did you get the boat?"

"A guy near the ferry dock rented it to us."

"Did he know where you were going?"

"He never asked."

"I'm assuming you were familiar with Casco Bay, had charts and a compass."

"What do I need those for? I could see the island. I set my GPS for it. Those rocks should have been marked."

"They are. On the chart." He looked sternly at Noah. "You have much to learn about boating in this bay and the ocean. Mariners use charts in unfamiliar waters. With no chart, you ran into rocks near this island, yes?"

"I guess so," Noah said reluctantly.

"Dad, Noah grew up on boats," Alex said, trying to change her dad's inquisition into a more positive approach.

"Once you are warm, we can take you to Ares island. Do you have anything with you, or is it all on the bottom of Casco Bay?" Alex asked.

"We sent our things on the ferry. We didn't want to be bothered with them on the boat."

Gus rolled his eyes and sighed. "Let's go. My boat is still in the water, and I'd like to get you there and return here before the storm that is cranking up hits."

Alex, knowing how disgusted her dad was with the ignorance of these two, went with him and Tony, hoping to keep him from lecturing the survivors. On their boat, her dad made a show of calling up the chart on his tablet computer, pointing out Rocky Cove and the note that there are submerged rocks there, especially at high tide. Then he told Alex, "Our course to where we can safely head for Ares Island is 10 degrees. Once we are here," he pointed to a spot on the chart, "I'll change course to 15 degrees, which will take us to the island." He turned to Alex and said, "Keep these two company while I get us there. They will be warmer in the cabin. Tony can help me navigate." A limousine from the hotel met them at the Landis Resort dock on Ares Island and took the two honeymooners to the resort.

The trip back to Gomes Island was rougher than going over, but they reached their dock with no mishaps, except being a little damp due to the spray from the waves. Alex helped the men get the boat prepared for the coming storm. Before they finished, the snow started falling in earnest. With the strong wind, it was hard for them to make their way back to the house.

Shaking off snow, they entered their house. In a disgusted voice, Gus said, "Darn fools. They were lucky. We found them because Tony wanted to see the island from the air. He spotted them in the water."

"Yes, they were lucky and incredibly naïve," Alex said. "Noah's boating experience, limited to an inland lake in the Ozarks where, I suspect, the waves never get over two feet, if that, left him woefully unprepared for the Atlantic."

Hanging up her coat, she said, "How about this storm? I wish Samantha were here to enjoy it."

Smiling at his daughter's change of the subject and realizing there was no reason to dwell on the rescue episode, he said to Alex, "You didn't get much time with Mia. It's only four o'clock, so why don't you spend the rest of the afternoon with her while Tony and I relax and watch a little football? That is, if you think you can make it there and back in the snow," he said teasingly.

"I think I can," Alex said, laughing. "The fence by the road will be visible even if the road is covered. I'll take a flashlight. I'll be home by five-thirty to make dinner."

"Your dad was pretty disgusted with those two, wasn't he?" Mr. Trumble greeted Alex as she entered their home to see Mia.

"That is an understatement. I imagine Tony and I will hear more about it tonight. It's good that guy is not a first officer assigned to him. He'd never get off the ground."

Hearing this exchange, Mia laughed. "Seems to me I remember a little episode when you overloaded a boat."

"Dad is a stickler where safety is concerned. But I learned my lesson and never violated it or any other safety policy again."

"Mia, I'd like to see your Mom. I hope these antics did not upset or tire her."

"On the contrary. She said that hearing your dad grilling that man was her best entertainment in months. And she wants to see you."

By the time Alex returned home, the snow and wind had increased. She was surprised to see her dad and Tony in the kitchen finishing the open-faced sandwiches.

Seeing her, Gus said, "Alex, pour yourself a drink or some wine, whatever you want, and then we'll all go to the living room while these cook." He popped the sandwiches into the preheated oven and set the timer.

That evening and night, the snow continued, and they woke up the next morning to a sunny, white world. There was no wind, but the temperature had fallen to the high teens. "Anyone brave enough for a walk?" Gus asked.

"Me," chorused Alex and Tony.

"Bundle up! Tony, I think you will fit into Nelson' heavy jacket that he leaves here."

The snow crackled under their feet as they left the house. "I can feel the cold in my nose," Alex laughed. "Look at the trees! We're lucky the wind has not yet blown the snow off."

As they walked, Gus lamented that his granddaughters were not there to enjoy the snow.

It was Sunday too soon, and Alex and Tony had to return to Rabbit Island, although Tony was looking forward to meeting his boys at O'Hare and flying back with them to

Rabbit Island.

After giving Alex a hug and kiss before she passed through security, Gus held Tony back. "Tony, I am delighted that you came with Alex. I hope you will have many more visits to our island. You've made Alex very happy. I haven't seen her this radiant since before David died, and that was 16 years ago. Thank you."

"Gus, I assure you, Alex has made me very happy too. How about visiting us in March?"

"We'll see," he replied, patting Tony on the back.

Tony met his sons at O'Hare just as they had planned. Alex stayed out of the way until Tony, with his sons, approached her and introduced them. Hunter, at 16, the oldest, shook her hand warmly, while Carter, who was 14, was more hesitant to meet her.

"It's nice to meet you both," Alex told them.

"Are you going to be my mother?" Carter asked in a concerned tone.

"You already have a mother. I'm just a good friend of your fathers. I will never take her place."

After the introductions, Alex suggested, "Tony, when we get on the plane, why don't you and Carter sit together, and I will sit with Hunter." It was not long before the plane to Rabbit Island was announced, and they joined the crowd lining up to board.

As they fastened their seatbelts, the Captain of the Blue Water flight approached Tony, "Captain Hamilton, I'm glad to see you on our little airline. I'd heard you left Worldwide Airways and were now running Rabbit Island airport. How do you like it?"

"It's been a challenge, but I'm enjoying it. It's nice to wake up in the same place every morning. Tonight, I'm bringing my sons to Rabbit Island for their first visit."

"You're in luck. The weather looks good, and we should

be early enough that I can circle the Island and give everyone a good view."

"The boys will enjoy that. By the way, rumor has it that some of the captains on Blue Water Air will be joining Worldwide Airways. Will you be one of them?

"Yes. This is my last stretch with Blue Water Air. And I better get it going!"

As promised, the captain gave everyone on board an aerial tour of Rabbit Island. "What do you do down there?" Carter asked his father.

"Well, I'm pretty busy at the airport, but there are some wonderful hiking trails in Rabbit Island State Park that I was planning to introduce you to. And, there is a problem I was hoping you could help me with. In my apartment, I need some shelves in the kitchen, but I don't know where to put them. I'm assuming you are still interested in being an architect."

"But Dad, that's not architecture."

"Perhaps not exactly, but you will learn a little about how to, or how not to, design buildings when you plan how to accomplish this. Usability is an important factor. Whoever designed my apartment seems to at times to have forgotten this. I suspect you will be able to see what I mean after you are here for a few days."

As they were landing, Tony could see Alex and Hunter very engaged in conversation. Hunter seemed more open to his relationship with Alex than Carter.

After deplaning, Alex said goodbye to Tony and the boys and went to her car in the employee parking lot. "By the way, Tony. You'd better plan some time with Miss Maggie. She knows your boys are here and will want to meet them."

"I know! She has invited us to dinner on Monday night. Will you be there?"

"Not this time." She looked at Hunter and Carter and said, "You boys don't know what a treat you are in for at Miss

Maggie's. A dinner that will rival any you have ever had."

"Carter eats like a horse," Hunter said. "Will there be enough food?"

Carter gave Hunter a playful punch on the arm and said, "You should talk. You eat more than me."

"Boys," Alex said, "There is always more than enough at Miss Maggie's. I suspect she will also send you home with food."

25 New Beginnings

When Alex saw Dr. Gould in the Clinic Monday morning, he asked, "How was your holiday with Tony and family?"

"It was interesting and a lot of fun."

"Knowing you, there must have been some excitement."

"Just a little. My dad and Tony found a couple of idiots floating in Casco Bay after their boat hit a submerged rock and broke up. My friend's dad and I rescued them."

"Alex, excitement follows you like your shadow. You are incorrigible," he laughingly said.

"Incidentally, my wife, Charlotte, is looking forward to a New Year's off the island. If there is anything you can't handle, I'm sure you will have no trouble getting transportation to either Crescent City General or Downstate," he said with a sly smile, adding, "Miss Maggie is not the only one glad to have you and Captain Hamilton back together. I don't want to lose you."

"At the beginning of February, we will have Ann Hooper too."

"Still learning, though."

"Yes, but we are all still learning. Have a great New Year's Eve." The doctor smiled and left as Alex went into a patient's room, thinking it was funny he had not asked about her meeting Tony's sons.

The Wednesday evening dinner, during which Alex

entertained Tony and his sons, was a success. Even Carter had warmed up to her. Of course, her prime rib dinner did not hurt. Tony smiled to himself at the thought. Despite missing Alex, he had enjoyed catching up on his sons' lives. After putting them on the one o'clock Blue Water flight New Year's Eve he had been a little blue, but cheered up at the thought he would be spending New Year's Eve with Alex.

Like the caring father and pilot he is, he checked the weather for the boys' flights and was relieved to find it good all along their route. Just before they closed the plane door on the California flight, Hunter texted them that the connection at O'Hare was easy, and they were on board the San Francisco plane.

Tony and Alex spent a quiet New Year's Eve, glad to be together again. Despite saying they wouldn't, they managed to stay up to watch the ball fall in Times Square. "I don't know why we do this," Tony said.

"Neither do I, but I love it! And tomorrow, we will welcome the New Year at Miss Maggie's with the Pauls, Brad Teaberry, Bert Nelson, and the Hoopers."

Their New Year's Day celebration was interrupted by an emergency call requiring Alex to go to the Clinic.

As she let the patients in, she said, "I'm Dr. Lawson, a nurse practitioner. What seems to be the problem?"

"I fell out of a tree," a young girl said, almost proudly. "And my arm hurts."

"Can I ask what you were doing in a tree?"

"My brother told me I couldn't climb it. He said I was too small."

"And, of course, you had to prove him wrong," Alex said with a small smile.

"Wouldn't you?"

"Probablly not unless I was very sure I could to it. Did your fall cause the arm to hurt?"

"Yes. My mother thinks it's broken."

"What do you think?"

"It hurts."

"What's your name?"

"Chloe Jasper."

"And how old are you?"

"Six," she said, proudly adding, "But I'll be seven in March."

Turning to the woman with Chloe, Alex said, "Are you Mrs. Jasper?"

"Yes. And the mother of the little girl who couldn't resist a dare," she said resignedly. "We are new to the island and have heard that there is excellent care here. This is my first visit to the Rabbit Island Clinic."

"Would you like me to take care of your daughter and then get you registered?"

"Yes. She was complaining on the way here."

"I'll start by taking an x-ray to see if the arm is broken."

Studying Chloe's x-rays, Alex could see a simple break near her wrist. Approaching the mother and daughter, Alex said, "Chloe and Mrs. Jasper, there is a break in the right arm near the growth plate at the wrist."

"Growth plate, what is that?" Mrs. Jasper asked.

"When a person is born, their entire body is small. The limbs lengthen by growing at each end. We call those ends growth plates. An untreated fracture at the growth plate can result in a limb that never reaches its full growth. Hence, it will be shorter than the other one. Fortunately, your daughter has a simple fracture, that is, although the bone is fractured, both parts are still in place."

"I don't want one arm shorter than the other. Can't it be fixed?" Chloe asked in a concerned voice.

"Yes, but you'll have to work with me. First, I'll do what we call stabilize your wrist. To do that, I will put your wrist and lower arm in a cast. That means you won't be able to bend your arm at the wrist. No climbing trees, no matter what your brother says." Alex told her, thinking how glad she was that only a few weeks ago she had prevailed on Dr. Gould to show her how to apply a cast. Now, she could treat the patient here, and they would not have to go to Crescent City General.

"If you do this, will the growth plates, as you call them, be okay?" Chloe asked in a solemn voice.

"One never promises, but the odds are excellent. The cast, however, carries its own set of instructions."

"Put the cast on and tell me what to do. I will do as you say." Suddenly, Chloe grinned, her seriousness forgotten, and added brightly, "Once it's on, can I have my friends sign it?"

Smiling, Alex said, "Of course. But only after it is thoroughly dry. Let's see, today is Thursday. If you are careful to keep it dry, it will be okay by Monday when you are back in school. But make sure your arm is fully supported when your friends sign, like on a desk."

"I will, I will," the little girl said, smiling.

"And keep it dry at all times. Don't even think of putting it into water," Alex smiled and added, "No matter what your brother says."

"I will do as you say, not listen to his dumb dares."

"That's the spirit!"

After casting the arm, as Alex registered Chloe, Mrs. Jasper told her, "I'm so glad you are here. You have taken very good care of us. We want to be your patients if there is room for new patients."

"We would be pleased to have you as our patients. I will give you some information about how to register your family members. It's easiest to do online. Is that okay with you?"

"Certainly." Mrs. Jasper laughed. "I didn't expect to have to deal with this so soon. We've only been on the island a month."

"Welcome to Rabbit Island!" Alex told her. "By the way, you need to bring Chloe back next week so we can check on her. Meanwhile, the arm will feel better if she keeps it elevated. I will prescribe a pill for her pain for a few days so she can sleep. She is a very brave young lady," Alex said, smiling at Chloe. "If the pain persists beyond a few days, come back and see us."

"How long will it take to heal?"

"About six weeks." Looking at Chloe, Alex told her, "If, Chloe, you stop letting your older brother challenge you. It's up to you to follow our instructions. Now, enjoy the rest of the day."

As they left, Alex said to herself, "I think we may see more of the young girl. Trying to keep up with Big Brother can be hazardous to her health. Let's hope none of the injuries are more serious than this. And that he doesn't push his luck showing off." Smiling, she locked the Clinic and went to join Tony at Miss Maggie's.

With Dr. Gould gone Alex was on call. The next day, with no calls on the answering machine, Tony suggested, "Why don't we go to Steve's for brunch?"

"That sounds like a good way to end the holidays. Do you think we can get a reservation?"

"Let's just go and take our chances."

Much to their surprise, Julie, the hostess and wife of the owner of Steve's Island Resort, seated them right away. Bringing them coffee, she said, "I've got some interesting news to tell you. Order your breakfast, and I'll tell you about it when I can."

"Oh," both Alex and Tony said in unison with puzzled looks on their faces.

Enjoying their brunch, Tony asked, "Alex, what did you think of my sons?"

"The short time I was lucky enough to be with them, I

enjoyed them. Your former wife has done a good job, although I know you were involved as much as you could be."

"I tried. But there was so much I missed. Although I talked with my ex-wife twice a week about the boys, and also with each of the boys."

"I got the impression they love you. You are lucky. Your former wife is cooperative and has not turned the boys against you. That too often happens."

"I know. But I hope to see more of them. She has agreed to let them spend the summer here. Hunter has earned his private pilot's license and is as crazy about flying as I was."

"Tony, you still are."

"Anyway, I can use him around the airport. We always need a plane washed, or taken out or put back into the hangar. I did that as a kid. It was how I earned my flying lessons."

"What about Carter?"

"He's interested in architecture. He solved a problem for me while he was here. He was able to get some corner shelves in a not-so-square corner. He also found out that the local school is having a class on elementary calculus this summer, and he met the requirements. So, he signed up for it. That should introduce him to a few of the kids on the island. He may be only fourteen, but he is mature for his age and hungry to learn. Sometimes I think he is more mature than Hunter," Tony said laughing.

When they were almost finished with their breakfast, Julie came over and sat down with them. After exchanging greetings she said, "During the holidays, I was in Austin, Texas, at an event to publicize our Rabbit Island Resort and, of course, our Island. There I saw a young lady, probably about sixteen or seventeen, who," Julie paused and looked directly at Alex, "was the spitting image of you. I thought I was seeing you as a teen."

At this news, Alex paled but asked, "What was her

name?"

"I never had a chance to speak to her, but I heard her mother call her Aurora."

"Interesting," Tony told Julie as Alex sat quietly.

"Perhaps her family will visit Rabbit Island, and you can see for yourself," Julie said, smiling as she got up to leave."

After Julie had gone, Tony said in a concerned voice, "Alex, you look like you've seen a ghost."

Her face rigid and pale, she replied, "Maybe I have." To Tony's quizzical look, she said, "Remember when I told you what happened when I was driving home after David was killed?"

"You had a stillborn baby."

"Tony, I'm sure the baby was not stillborn but stolen from me. This girl Julie saw is my baby's age."

"Are you sure?"

"Yes," Alex said defiantly. "I thought you said you believed me when I told you."

"I did, and I still do, but for Julie to see this young girl and think of you, could that be just a coincidence?"

"I guess it could be. But the geographic location fits. I wonder if I want that family to visit. The entire thing is still painful. I don't know what I would do if she were my stolen daughter."

"Let's not put the cart before the horse," Tony said with an understanding tone. "Before we go home, let's take a drive around the island. The snow last night left everything with a coat of white. It will be beautiful and maybe help you feel better. The snow won't last long."

Working hard to forget what Julie had told them, Alex tried to appreciate the scenery and said in a monotone, "This is my first winter on Rabbit Island. I guess I should appreciate what we have here." Turning to Tony, she added more enthusiastically, "Especially my life here and with you."

"Alex, whatever happens, I'll support you."

"And whatever was, was, and is behind me. I've moved on," Alex said unconvincingly.

Hoping to cheer Alex up, and wanting to ask her something, Tony drove to the Rabbit Island State Park and parked the car. "Come on, get out and come with me."

Alex half-heartedly got out of the car and caught up with Tony, who was headed for the overlook of Lake Nanabush in the center of the park. Taking her hand, he said, "Look at the mist rising out of the lake and the frost it has generated on the lower trees."

Pulling herself together, Alex said, "It is beautiful. We're lucky to live in such a magical place."

"And have each other," Tony said as he slowly put his arms around her, locked her in a bear hug, and kissed her. Releasing her, he looked at her and said, "Alex, I know that the information that Julie gave you is upsetting, and I will support you in whatever you want to do about it."

"Probably best to forget it. I just hope I can."

"Alex, there is something I didn't want to ask until you met my sons. They are a part of me and always will be. But now you have met them and I think like them. And I don't know if this is the right time to ask after Julie told you about the young girl she saw in Texas, but I have to know." He turned her to face him, put both hands on her shoulders and asked, "Alex, will you marry me? "

"Do your boys know that you were going to ask me?"

"Yes, and they are in favor of it. When I told them Hunter said, "What took you so long dad? And let's hope she says yes."

Still looking at her Tony said, "Will you? Before you answer, know that if you marry me you will gain two stepsons."

Forgetting her former mood, she wrapped her arms

around him, pulled him close and said, "Yes I will marry you. I wouldn't accept if your sons weren't part of the deal. However, there are a few conditions."

"What are they?"

"I will not change my name professionally. Can you live with that?"

"Alex, I would not expect you to. You have a career and are known by your name. I would have suggested it if you hadn't.

"However, socially, I will be happy to be Mrs. Anthony Alexander Hamilton."

Smiling, Tony said, "Alex, you have made me the happiest man in the world."

"Tony, the feeling is mutual. And in the bargain, I'm gaining two stepsons. You can't beat that!" She laughed. "And let's share our happiness with Miss Maggie."

"I think she will be delighted. Probably want to give you away."

"No doubt, but that privilege is reserved for my dad."

"Would you like a Valentine's Day wedding?"

"Nothing would please me more. I guess that I'm a bit of a Romantic at heart."

"You may deprive Miss Maggie of walking you down the aisle, but I suspect she will take the task of planning the wedding and reception from you. The other alternative is for us to elope."

Laughing, Alex said, "You do go right to the crux of the matter, don't you? I hope Hunter and Carter will be able to come."

"I think it can be arranged."

Fiction Books by Linda Q. Thede

The Canoe's Secret – 2020

Rabbit Island Nurse Practitioner Series

Miss Maggie's Quest 2024

Dangerous Boxes 2024

If you enjoyed this book, a review on Amazon would be greatly appreciated.

ABOUT THE AUTHOR

 Linda Q. Thede's authoring career began with a popular non-fiction book teaching students about nursing informatics, and a 2012 winner of the *American Journal of Nursing's* Book of the Year award. For 10 years she edited a popular feature in *CIN: Computers Informatics Nursing*. More recently, she expanded her genre to fiction with her first novel, *The Canoe's Secret*. This is her fourth fiction book and the third in a series. For many years, she sailed on the Great Lakes with her late husband, which gave her the idea for the fictional island, Rabbit Island. She lives in a Continuing Care Retirement Community near Charlotte, NC, where she edits their newsletter and serves as a Train Host on Amtrak. She has three children and seven grandchildren.

www.ingramcontent.com/pod-product-compliance
Lightning Source LLC
Chambersburg PA
CBHW071501170626
46811CB00007B/2672